VEILED

JEFF STRAND

ISBN: 9798395671912

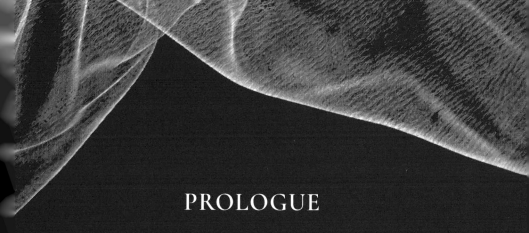

PROLOGUE

D irk got a very strong "this chick is crazy" vibe from the woman who sat down next to him, but it wasn't strong enough for him to move to another stool.

She was hot but clearly out of her element in this dark seedy bar. Her makeup was applied strangely, like she'd put a great deal of care into it but didn't really know what she was doing. She seemed uncomfortable in her tight cleavage-baring blouse—her hands kept moving as if she was unconsciously trying to cover up. When she'd asked if this seat was taken, her alluring smile was a bit twitchy.

Of course, the critical element was that she was hot. She was maybe thirty, so she was a few years older than him. If she'd been, say, mid-thirties or forties he would've been grossed out, but thirty was totally cool. Though he wouldn't devote *too* much effort to hitting on her, he'd certainly buy her a drink and see if he could make anything happen.

"I'm Alice," she said, extending her hand.

"Dirk," he said, shaking it.

"Am I bothering you?"

"Not at all. Can I buy you a drink?"

She nodded. "What's good here?"

"I'm having whiskey."

"Okay, that's what I'll have. Actually, no, I should just have beer. Light beer. Any brand."

Dirk grinned and ordered her drink. He was pretty good at figuring out people's stories, and this was hers: Her boyfriend had just cheated on her, and she'd thought, "*If he can do it, so can I!*" She'd never had a one-night stand in her life and felt awkward about making it happen. She'd most likely regret it in the morning, but what happened in the morning wasn't Dirk's concern.

"I can tell this isn't your thing," he told her. "You can relax. I don't bite." In many past experiences, he would pause and then add "...hard" with a chuckle, but the last woman he'd hit on had informed him it was a cheesy, overused line, so he'd removed it from the rotation.

"You're right, it's not," Alice admitted. "I'm *so* out of my element here it isn't even funny."

The bartender set a beer in front of her. She wiped off the condensation with a napkin, then took a quick sip. She smiled at Dirk. "It tastes good. Thank you. This was nice of you."

"What is your element?"

"Pretty much any place but a bar."

"So, like, the opera and shit like that?"

"Maybe not *that* classy. Coffee shops and libraries, I guess. Do you like to read?"

"Oh, sure, sure," Dirk lied.

"Don't worry, I won't quiz you on your favorite books."

"You'd rather be at a coffee shop. What brings you here, then?"

Alice shrugged.

"You can tell me. I'm a friendly ear."

Alice took a drink of her beer. "We're both adults. There's nothing wrong with going after what we want, right?" She took another drink. Then one more. "I'm here to get laid."

Dirk nodded his approval. "That's very direct. I like it."

"What about you?"

"I was here to get a couple of drinks, but getting laid would be a great byproduct." He suddenly wondered if he'd used "byproduct" correctly. If this lady hung out in libraries, messing up a word might be a turnoff.

"Then it's win-win," she said.

"It sure is. Well, if you're on the prowl for a lover, I guess I should start trying to be charming."

"You're good. You've achieved the minimum amount of necessary charm."

"Glad to hear it," said Dirk. "Can I ask you a question?"

"Sure."

"Is this a revenge thing?"

"What do you mean?"

"Are you getting back at somebody? It's okay if you are. Not a deal-breaker for me at all. I totally approve of revenge hookups."

Alice thought about that for a moment. "Yes," she said. "I think of it as 'fairness,' but revenge works, too."

"Cheating boyfriend?"

"Got it in one guess."

"What an idiot."

"Eh. You don't know the circumstances. Maybe she was a gorgeous eighteen-year-old with gigantic—" Alice used her hands to mime huge breasts, though it amused Dirk that she seemed uncomfortable saying an actual word for them.

"Even so, he's an idiot. Even if it was two gorgeous eighteen-year-olds with gigantic boobs, he's a complete dumbass."

"That's sweet."

"I can be sweet."

"Do you have a place we can go?"

Dirk nodded. "I do."

"Should we head off? I still have most of my beer left, but we could give it to somebody, or leave it. I don't want to rush us out of here. I was just thinking that if we've both made our decision, we might as well get to it."

"You're not going to axe murder me, are you?" Dirk asked.

Alice laughed. "Of course not."

Dirk was suddenly less convinced that Alice was not an axe-murderer.

Oh, he was still going to take her back to his apartment, but he wouldn't let her sleep over, and he'd watch her carefully if she asked where he kept his kitchen knives.

"CAN I GET YOU A DRINK?" HE ASKED, BUT SHE'D ALREADY TAKEN OFF her shirt and gone into the bedroom. She hadn't even asked for a quick tour, not that there was much of his apartment to show off. For somebody so shy and awkward, she was sure ready to get right down to it.

He followed her into the bedroom, where she was unfastening her bra. "I guess this is probably your job," she said, tossing the bra aside. "Figured I'd save you some work."

"Much appreciated." Dirk had pretty decent luck with the ladies, but he'd never encountered anything like this. He couldn't really be flattered by it; he suspected that her criteria for a sexual partner tonight was a penis, any penis. Still, he was happy about his good fortune and immediately began removing his own clothes.

Alice finished before him. She looked pretty good naked,

though there were stretch marks and a faint C-section scar. No way was he getting into any kind of serious relationship with somebody who had kids. Not that there was any chance of this becoming an actual relationship anyway—she was, after all, obviously crazy. He might not be averse to a second or third hook-up, depending on how this one went, but then he'd go back to his younger girlfriends with their tighter bodies.

She was wearing a necklace that had a silver eyeball pendant, about the size of a peanut M&M. It kind of creeped him out. He didn't say anything, because if she was this horny, he didn't want to mess things up by criticizing her jewelry.

After he removed his socks, he put his arms around her and kissed her lips. She flinched a bit but returned the kiss.

"Don't be nervous," he told her.

"I'm not nervous."

"Yes, you are."

"Yes, I am. Sorry."

"It's nothing to apologize for. I'm just saying there's no need to worry. We're only doing what you want. If you ask me to stop, I'll stop. It's going to be fine. We're going to have a great time."

She kissed him. Within seconds, the tentative kisses were gone, and the two of them were full-on making out. She ran her hand down his side—which tickled—then curled her fingers around his penis and gently stroked him. Wow. She wasn't messing around.

Alice took Dirk's hand and placed it on her breast. Dirk preferred the feel of fake ones, but this was quite pleasing to the touch.

They made out like this for a couple of minutes. She never stopped stroking him. Though her technique was okay, his penis wasn't responding at all.

She dropped to her knees and took him into her mouth.

She was less skilled with her mouth than her hand, but still, a hot chick was going down on him less than half an hour after they'd first met, and no money had exchanged hands. He suddenly wondered if she was a prostitute who would demand payment afterward, but no—she was too nervous to be a hooker. And besides, if they hadn't agreed on a price beforehand, he could simply send her away.

He placed his hand on top of her head, closed his eyes, and just enjoyed the sensation.

His dick still wasn't cooperating.

This had never happened to him before. Oh, sure, he'd been tired and simply not in the mood, especially with his bitchy ex-girlfriend, Tina, but he'd never had a problem getting it up when he was actively rooting for things to happen. Why wasn't he getting hard? What was wrong with him?

It was obvious. Alice was being too aggressive, and there was something very much "off" about her. Consciously, he liked having her down there, doing what she was doing, but deep in his brain a little voice was saying, *This is kind of messed up,* and it was preventing blood from flowing to his groin.

Thinking about his erectile dysfunction was the easiest way to ensure that it would continue. Yet he couldn't *not* think about it! What else was he supposed to think about?

She picked up her pace and even though he could only see the top of her head, Dirk could tell she was getting frustrated.

After another minute or so, he was pretty sure his dick had completely failed him, and no amount of head-bobbing on her part was going to fix the issue. Since this was all new to him, he wasn't sure when to officially pull the plug. Now? Should he give it a couple more minutes, just in case? Should she be the one to call it quits? How did this process work?

She pulled away from him and looked up. "It's okay," she said. "Just relax."

"I'm relaxed. I'm just...I'm sorry."

Alice smiled, though she was obviously making a conscious decision to do so. "You're the one who told me not to be nervous."

"I know, I know. This has never happened to me."

"You're a virgin?"

"What? No. God, no. I normally have to work a little harder to get laid. Nobody has ever been as, y'know, accommodating as you."

Alice nodded. It suddenly concerned Dirk that her teeth were so close to the sensitive skin of his genitalia. "Then let's slow it down," she said. "We'll watch a TV show and try again later."

DIRK HAD BEEN BINGE-WATCHING *PARKS & RECREATION*, AND ALICE said she didn't care what they watched, so that's what Dirk put on. They sat side by side in his bed. About ten minutes into the episode, Alice began to gently rub his leg. Before the episode was over, she'd moved to his penis again. By the time the end credits rolled, he still wasn't responding to her affection.

"Maybe this was a bad idea," he said.

"*No*," she said, eyes wide. She sounded frantic and, to be honest, a little scary. "No," she said, much more calmly. "I don't want to go looking for somebody else. It was hard enough for me to work up the nerve to do it the first time."

"There are plenty of dating apps."

Alice shook her head. "Please, Dirk. I really need this."

"Why?"

"Why do you think?"

"I don't know. Is it that you're so horny you can't stand it? Are you insanely desperate to get revenge on your boyfriend?" Dirk had been so excited about taking Alice home that it hadn't occurred to him she might throw this one-night stand into her boyfriend's face.

The dude might have a shotgun. And he could see Alice beaming and saying, "*Oh, my dear sweet love, you killed for me!*" and taking him back.

He really needed for Alice not to be in his apartment anymore.

Alice removed her hand from his lap. "I apologize if I came off as too needy. That wasn't my intention. I've had a rough couple of days, and I thought this would make me feel better. An online hookup isn't an option—I don't want to get stabbed or strangled. All I wanted was to meet a nice guy and go home with him so I wouldn't feel so ugly and useless."

Oh shit. Was she going to cry?

He had no idea what he'd do if she cried.

Please, please, please don't let her start bawling, he thought.

She took a deep breath. No tears flowed...yet.

"Let me stay," she said, speaking quietly. "I need the release. I'm not going to bring any drama into your life, I swear. I just need this."

"Yeah, all right," said Dirk. "If it's about an orgasm, I can take care of you, no problem. Here, lie on your back."

"That's not necessary."

"You sure? I'm happy to do it. I'm good at it. Nobody has ever complained."

"It never really does anything for me. Not my thing. I want you inside of me."

Dirk was kind of relieved. He'd go down on a woman if she asked—it was only fair—but it definitely wasn't his favorite activity in the world. Still, it would've been nice to make her come and send her away.

"So what do you want to do?" he asked.

"We'll wait it out. You *are* attracted to me, right?"

"Uh-huh."

"It'll happen. I came on too strong. I may have even been

creepy; I'll admit it. Let's sit back, watch some more TV, and let things move at a natural pace. How's that sound?"

"Sounds good," Dirk said.

They watched five more episodes. Though it was Dirk's favorite show (this was his third time watching the entire series), he didn't laugh as much as he normally did, even when the other characters were mean to Jerry. Truthfully, he just wanted Alice to go home, but it was hard to kick a naked woman out of his bed. And if she stayed, he might be able to redeem himself with a mighty erection and erase the memory of this debacle.

"Why don't we go to sleep?" she said. "Try again in the morning?"

Dirk most assuredly did not want to sleep with her. That was a good way to wake up with his penis in her hand...while she was in another room.

But he'd be safe as long as he didn't actually fall asleep, right? She couldn't overpower him. And he might be ready for action in the morning.

As he brushed his teeth, he wondered if he was nuts for not simply taking her by the arm and gently walking her to his front door. Yeah, he probably was. He definitely was.

Oh well. It would all be worth it if he was able to get aroused. He'd bang her like she'd never been banged before. She'd be begging for mercy. She wouldn't be able to walk straight for a week.

He climbed back into bed and shut off the light. She didn't snuggle against him.

It was difficult for Dirk to calculate the passage of time while he was lying in bed in the dark, but at some point he heard her sniffle. And then she was softly weeping.

He wanted to say something, but...actually, no, he didn't want to say anything. He wanted to lie there and pretend he was asleep until she stopped.

He opened his eyes. Sunlight streamed through his bedroom window.

Crap! He'd fallen asleep!

He looked over. Alice lay on her side, facing away from him. Okay, good. His throat hadn't been slashed, he hadn't been tied to the bed, and if Alice had stolen anything while he was asleep, it wasn't as if she had many places to hide it. Most importantly, he hadn't been castrated. That was good.

And...

Dirk had never been so happy to see morning wood in his life. He quickly reached over and shook her. "Alice? Alice...?"

She groaned and rolled toward him. Dirk tossed the blanket aside. He suddenly worried that she might say, *"Let me wake up first, for God's sake,"* as would any normal woman if he shook her awake and exposed his erect penis. But considering last night's challenges, he wasn't sure his morning boner would last long enough for him to bring her a cup of coffee first.

She yawned, rubbed her eyes, then snapped awake. He'd never seen such a smile when a woman gazed at his crotch. Although he had to admit, it wasn't so much a *delighted* smile as a *relieved* smile.

He opened the drawer and took out a condom. Alice straddled his legs as he tore at the wrapper. After a couple of failed attempts, she snatched the condom out of his hands and ripped it open with her teeth.

"Here," she said, handing it back. She didn't actually say, "Hurry!" but it was implied.

He unrolled the condom over his still-firm-thank-God penis. Without even waiting for him to move his hand, she guided him inside of her.

Oh, yeah. She felt great. He figured he'd let her ride him for a couple of minutes, then take her from behind and violently pound away until...

Shit, was he getting close already?

Alice was only on her third bounce, and he was hurtling toward the opposite problem as the one he experienced last night. How much sexual dysfunction was he going to endure? He desperately tried to think of something else, like baseball, his grandmother, or the fact that Alice might murder him afterward, but it did no good. He cried out in pleasure.

Damn. He hoped she didn't tell anybody.

Alice climbed off him. She didn't look the least bit disappointed.

"Thank you," she said.

"I can wash up real quick, and we can go again," Dirk insisted.

She smiled. "No, that's fine. You were a champ."

"Did you come?"

"Sure."

She got out of bed and gathered her clothes. This was one strange chick. Why wasn't she upset?

His stomach clenched in a moment of panic as he wondered if her whole plan was to get pregnant. But, no, the condom was still intact. He got out of bed, went into the bathroom, and removed it, feeling very confused.

When he returned, she was mostly dressed.

"Sorry I was so quick," he said.

"Not a problem at all."

"Would it offend you if I said this whole thing was kind of weird?"

"No. It *is* kind of weird." She bit her lip as if lost in thought for a moment. "I can tell you now, but...you know what? Forget it. Thank you for the beer. It was very good. I wish you all the best in everything you do in the future."

"Okay."

She finished buttoning her blouse, gave him a kiss on the cheek, then left.

Dirk just stood there for a minute. Then he walked around his apartment, checking to see if anything valuable was missing. As far as he could tell, she hadn't stolen anything.

Very, very strange.

Oh well. He'd technically gotten laid, even if there'd been plenty of humiliation involved, and he hadn't woken up to her sawing off his limbs. He supposed he'd simply chalk it up to "some chicks are batshit crazy" and move on with his life.

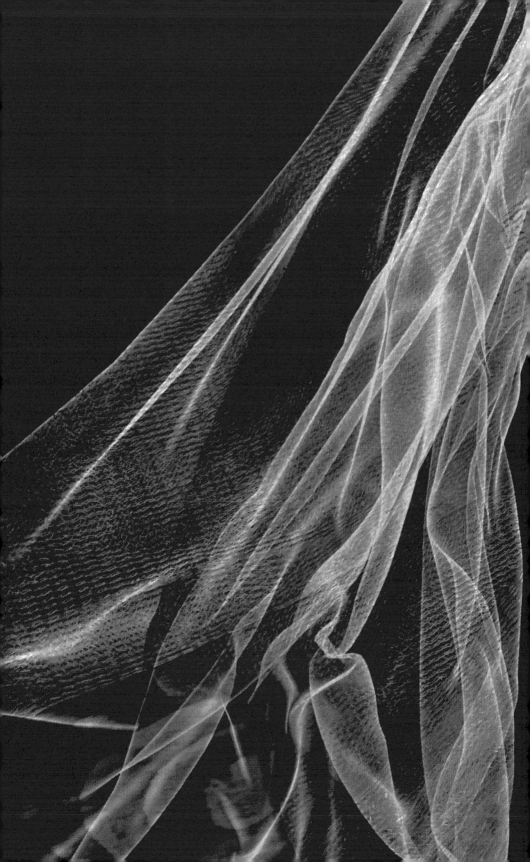

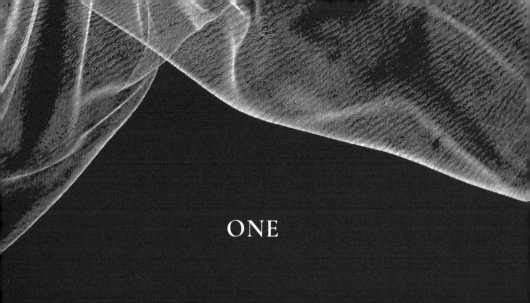

ONE

This was Nate Sommer's third time being mugged, and he had to admit, it did get easier.

The first time, four years ago, he'd been so scared that he wet his pants. The mugger had curled his lip in disgust, and Nate almost thought he'd pull the trigger simply to spare him a lifetime of shame. He'd quickly handed over his wallet and, because he was so flustered, thanked the mugger. Then he'd tried to make it home without anybody seeing his soaked pants and almost succeeded.

The second time, last year, he'd also been terrified, but he got through the experience without emptying his bladder or inappropriately thanking the criminal. He'd started carrying what he called his "mug wallet," which contained fake credit cards and forty bucks. It was a good idea, unless you got mugged immediately after withdrawing a large amount of cash from an ATM, which is what happened.

The third time, occurring right now, was a bit different. The mugger had a knife instead of a gun. His hand trembled, and his demand that Nate "hand over your fuckin' wallet before I fuckin' stab you, motherfucker" sounded like somebody who was trying too hard rather than speaking the words in his heart.

Nate felt like he could take him.

He was not one hundred percent sure of this. He was ninety percent sure. That left a ten percent chance that he could find himself lying on the sidewalk, covered in blood, with the handle of a knife jutting out of his belly. He didn't want that.

He should probably hand over his wallet. He'd left his mug wallet at home, because it made perfect sense that if he brought it the last three hundred times, he'd get mugged the one time he forgot it. Fate was an asshole.

Nate was reasonably tall, six foot one. The mugger was four or five inches shorter. Nate was in good physical shape. The mugger was practically emaciated. Nate was freshly caffeinated. The mugger seemed to be going through withdrawal symptoms. The only advantage the mugger had in a physical altercation was the knife, which, admittedly, was a pretty big advantage. Still...

"You gonna give me your fuckin' wallet or not?" asked the mugger, voice quivering.

Nate punched him in the nose.

The mugger's head flew back. Nate couldn't believe he'd really done it. He wasn't typically an "act on instinct" kind of guy. Normally he would have carefully weighed the pros and cons of punching a mugger in the face, perhaps composing a related graph in his mind before doing it.

The mugger let out of howl of pain, dropped the knife, and cupped his hands over his bleeding nose. Nate kicked the knife out of the way, though it struck the brick building they were standing next to and didn't go very far.

Though Nate was not a violent man by any stretch of the imagination, he couldn't really say that the situation was resolved as long as the mugger remained upright. So he punched him in the stomach, as hard as he could. The mugger doubled over, vomited, and dropped to his knees. Nate considered kicking him in the head, but decided he posed no real threat for now, and it would just be mean.

"*You fuckin' suck!*" the mugger informed him.

Nate took out his cell phone and dialed 911.

"*You heartless piece of shit!*" the mugger continued.

"How am I heartless? You tried to steal my wallet. You threatened to kill me. You're the bad guy." The mugger didn't answer. "I asked you a question: How am I heartless?"

Rather than explaining his rationale, he began to cry.

The mugger remained sprawled on the sidewalk until the police arrived. After they carted him away, the cop who took Nate's statement informed him that he really should have just given the man his wallet instead of punching him, and Nate agreed that, yes, though it had all turned out okay, it had been a foolish move. After all, there'd been that one in ten chance that he'd be dead or dying right now. It had been stupid. Truly stupid. Though he couldn't deny it felt pretty good.

"Can I keep the knife as a souvenir?" he asked the cop.

"No. You may not."

WHEN NATE GOT BACK TO HIS APARTMENT, HE TOOK A BAG OF ICE out of the freezer, poured it into a plastic bowl, added cold water, and then submerged his punching hand in it. It was really sore.

He stood at the kitchen counter and had a few minutes of what he assumed was post-traumatic stress disorder, where it occurred to him that some guy had been ready to *stab him to death*. He could have died tonight! He could be dead right now!

He should've just handed over his wallet. So he would've had to cancel a couple of credit cards and get a new driver's license. Big deal. He had a world of entertainment on his phone to occupy him while he stood in line at the DMV. He was lucky to be alive to beat himself up over how reckless he'd been.

Nobody had been around to record it, so he didn't even get a viral video out of it.

He checked his phone with his free hand and saw he'd missed a call from his friend Josh. They'd met several years ago in college, where they were both Fine Arts majors. Now they were both servers at the same Tex-Mex restaurant.

Nate called him back.

"Hey, what's going on?" Josh asked.

"Not much. Punched a mugger in the face and broke his nose."

"Nice. So are you busy tomorrow night?"

"No, why?"

"Remember Stacey?"

"No."

"Yes, you do."

"I guess you're the expert on what I remember."

"I've been talking to her on that dating site."

"Does she have purple streaks in her hair?"

"Yeah."

"Okay. I didn't know her name was Stacey."

"I told you that."

"I don't take notes during our conversations."

"Anyway, her name is Stacey."

"Gotcha," said Nate. "By the way, I wasn't making up the thing about breaking the mugger's nose. He tried to steal my wallet at knifepoint, and I punched him in the face."

"Was he tiny?"

"He was smaller than me, but he wasn't a third-grader or anything. He was a fully mature adult. With a knife. A real knife."

"You should've just given him your wallet," said Josh. "You could have gotten stabbed."

"I know."

"Anyway, back to Stacey."

"You don't believe me, do you?"

"I believe that *you* believe it, and that's all that matters."

"Asshole. I'll get a copy of the police report."

"You're just determined not to talk about Stacey, aren't you?"

"Tell me Stacey's life story. Start at conception."

"We've been talking online, and we did a couple of video chats, but I haven't completely convinced her that I'm not a rapist. What I've discovered is that first dates are way more fun when nobody thinks they're going to get raped. She's willing to go out tomorrow night, but she wants to bring her friend along, and you'd be joining us."

"So a blind date."

"Yeah."

Nate shrugged, even though Josh couldn't see him do it. "Okay."

"Cool. Thanks. Hey, don't tell her about the mugger. Even if you're telling the truth, it sounds like a lie."

"What if she asks why my hand is swollen?"

"Hide that hand. You don't want her wondering why it's swollen."

"You owe me one."

"No, I don't. I got you a date. We're going to have a nice dinner and then go bowling. If anything, you owe me."

"My hand is dunked in a bowl of ice water now. Bowling is the last thing I want to do."

Josh was silent for a moment. "The mugging thing is bullshit, right?"

"No! I broke his nose! I might have to testify against him in court. Why would I make that up? Since when do I have any reason to try to impress you?"

"Oh my God! Are you okay?"

"I told you. I hurt my hand."

"Are you okay otherwise?"

"Yes. I'm emotionally fragile, but I'm fine."

"Do you need me to come over?"

"No."

"I can be there in twenty minutes."

"No."

"If you change your mind, no matter how late, give me a call. Maybe bowling isn't a good idea. But Stacey said she loves bowling. That's one of the reasons she replied to my message. Still, she'll understand. She can't expect you to go bowling with a deformed hand. What good movies are playing now?"

"You know what, bowling's fine," said Nate. "If the swelling isn't down by tomorrow evening, I'll just watch."

"You sure?"

"I'm sure."

"Thanks. I'll talk to you tomorrow."

"Good night."

"G'night."

Nate disconnected the call and pulled his hand out of the ice water. The swelling had already gone down quite a bit. He was certainly in better shape than the mugger.

He was no fan of blind dates, but he didn't mind doing a favor for Josh, and he had no real horror stories from his past experiences. Typically, they ended with a friendly hug and no plans to meet again. He definitely wasn't looking for a girlfriend. Maybe in his thirties he'd want to settle down, but at twenty-six, he enjoyed his lifestyle of doing whatever he wanted, whenever he wanted.

Right now, for example, he wanted to work on his play.

It was a two-act comedy called *Frank, Frank, & Frank*, the funniest thing he'd ever written. Heartfelt, but not sappy. Deep, but not pretentious. He'd had a one-act comedy produced a couple of years ago, an experience that had been rewarding in every way, except financially. He didn't expect this one to be lucrative either, but he was damned proud, even though it still needed a lot of work.

Nobody knew he was working on a new play. Josh knew he was working on *something*, but Nate didn't like to talk about projects before they were done. It wasn't out of superstition or anything like that; he'd just found that, described aloud, his ideas tended to sound really stupid. Sharing them with others made him paranoid he was wasting his time on crap.

He was extremely confident this wasn't crap, though.

He worked on it for a couple hours, then watched TV.

NATE'S HAND WAS FINE THE NEXT MORNING. HE HAD THE DAY OFF, so he decided it was long past time to give his apartment a thorough cleaning. Not that he imagined for a second he'd be bringing his blind date back to his place. It was simply that he'd let things slide recently, in terms of not being a complete disgusting vile slob, and it was time to correct that.

He cranked up the music as loud as he could without his uptight neighbor complaining and began his cleaning frenzy. There was an alarming amount of candy in his couch cushions, and he couldn't explain how a lost shoe ended up under the sink, but, overall, there were no chilling discoveries.

A few hours later, including frequent breaks to check social media, the apartment was finished. Tidy. Beautiful. It would stay that way for at least a couple of days.

Then he showered and got dressed. For his attire, he went with "dapper while acknowledging he was going to a bowling alley." Jeans and a dark blue shirt. He checked himself in the mirror, saw no grotesque flaws in his appearance, and headed off.

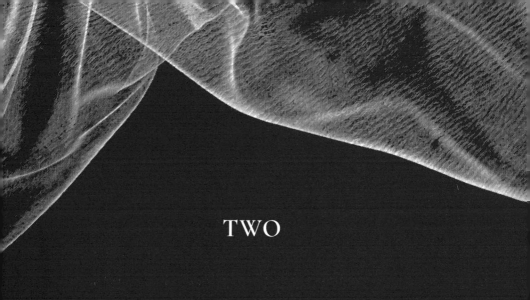

TWO

The four of them sat in a booth while the server prepared guacamole tableside. They were at a Tex-Mex restaurant —not the one where they worked, a better one on the other side of Atlanta. Given the option, Nate probably wouldn't have elected to have dinner at a place that served the same kind of food that surrounded him forty hours a week, but apparently Stacey was a big fan of tableside guac.

Josh and Stacey had hit it off immediately. They weren't exactly snuggling, but they were certainly sitting closer than the spacious booth required. Stacey was giggly without being annoying. Nate hoped that after a couple of dates, she'd be comfortable enough to stop trying to hide her obvious intelligence.

Gretchen, Nate's date, was not giggly.

From a purely facial construction standpoint, she was beautiful. In fact, she may have been the most physically attractive woman he'd ever been on a date with. But her supermodel looks were far overshadowed by her sullen demeanor. Gretchen did not want to be in this restaurant, and possibly not in this city, state, country, or planet. He suspected the vast majority of people she met filled her with sheer seething hatred.

Nate was actually kind of attracted to women who weren't fans of humanity, but there had to be an element of wit and snark to their disdain. It wasn't any fun if she just sat there wishing everybody around her was dead.

Josh made a guacamole-themed joke. Stacey laughed and playfully punched him on the shoulder. Nate noticed she used this opportunity to scoot an inch closer to him. If he scooted an inch closer to Gretchen, he was pretty sure she'd turn toward him and hiss.

The server finished making their appetizer, and everybody grabbed some chips and dug in. Gretchen ate, but without outward evidence that she tasted any flavor.

"Do you have any pets?" Nate asked her.

She shook her head. "I don't like pets."

"Pets in general?"

"Correct."

"How do you not like pets in general?"

Josh glared at him. *Don't you dare start an argument and mess this up for me, you son of a bitch. Don't you do it. This is going well for me. Bite your tongue. Bite it.*

"I just don't like them," Gretchen said.

"Are you allergic?"

"I wish."

"Do you like goldfish?"

"No. I don't like pets. Or talking about pets."

"All right, fair enough," said Nate. He could understand thinking that cats were stuck-up jerks, or dogs needed to just chill out, or even that hermit crabs were nightmarish creatures from Hell. But an overall dislike of pets, all pets, was baffling to him. He supposed you could take the approach that animals were beautiful creatures who deserved to roam free upon the earth, rather than be imprisoned indoors by human masters, but he was pretty sure Gretchen would happily whack a cow in the head with a hammer, given the opportunity. She simply wasn't into the idea of pets, like a sociopath.

The meal improved when he stopped trying to converse with her, leaving Gretchen to nibble her cheese quesadilla and glower.

This sucked. He could be sitting two tables over. A blonde woman, maybe thirty years old, sat alone. She was reading a paperback book while she ate the free chips and salsa. When she noticed Nate looking at her—not staring, just looking—she smiled. Nate immediately looked away. Gretchen was a miserable black hole from which no happiness escaped, but still, she was his date, and he didn't want to be rude.

He noticed the woman kept glancing at him throughout the meal. She wasn't even trying to hide it. It was almost as if there was an unspoken message: *I can tell your date is going horribly, so feel free to switch tables if you want to end the torture.*

He didn't switch tables, of course.

The woman lifted a taco to him in salute as the four of them left the restaurant.

Bowling was just as unpleasant. Oh, not for Josh and Stacey— they laughed and cheered each other on, and Stacey let Josh give her frequent helpful tips she obviously didn't need. Their interaction fell short of him actually pressing against her as he demonstrated proper bowling technique, but she was definitely over her fears about meeting him in real life. Gretchen remained sour-faced throughout the experience, even though she was the best bowler in the group, and the violence of her ball brutally smashing into pins should have soothed her.

After the second game, the ladies went to the restroom together. Nate and Josh sat and took off their bowling shoes.

"Could you do me favor?" Josh asked.

"I've been doing you a favor all night."

"Could you take Gretchen home? Stacey was her ride."

"Things going that well, huh?"

Josh grinned. "Not the way you're thinking. But we were gonna go out for ice cream, and we thought it might be more fun if it was just the two of us."

"Yeah, all right, I can take her home."

"Jeez, don't sound so excited."

"Why *would* I be excited?"

Josh seemed surprised by the question. "She's gorgeous."

"Not on the inside. Haven't you noticed how awful she is? She doesn't even like pets."

"I guess I was paying more attention to Stacey."

"I'll drive Gretchen home, but you're basically worse than Hitler for making me do it."

"Thanks, dude. I'll cover a shift for you if you ever need it."

"Yeah, yeah, whatever."

GRETCHEN SCOWLED DURING THE ENTIRE DRIVE. NATE ASKED WHAT kind of music she wanted to listen to, but she said that she didn't care for music, so they drove in silence.

"Well, thank you for a lovely evening," Nate said as he pulled up in front of her apartment complex.

"Are you coming in?"

"Excuse me?"

"Are you coming up to my apartment?"

"I, uh, hadn't planned on it, no."

"Seriously?"

"I'm really surprised you asked. I thought you'd leap out of the car before I even came to a complete stop."

Gretchen glared at him. "I suffered through this whole night, and you're not even going to put out?"

"I honestly didn't know that was your end goal. You probably could've paved the road to that a little better."

"How many goddamn signals did I need to send?"

"Sorry."

Gretchen opened the door, uttered a homophobic slur, then got out of the car. He braced himself for her to slam the door with enough force to shatter all the windows, but she closed it normally and then stormed off.

Nate wondered if she would've been impressed by his story about punching out the mugger.

He drove home, worked some more on his play, and went to sleep.

NATE DIDN'T HAVE TO BE AT WORK UNTIL THREE, SO HE SLEPT IN. He put on clothes that were clean enough for a day with no planned social interaction, then opened the refrigerator. It was a barren wasteland. He hated grocery shopping, but he'd reached the point where condiments were being considered as main courses, so it was time to suck it up and go.

He pushed his cart through the aisles, adding six boxes of macaroni and cheese, a large bag of potato chips, three boxes of breakfast cereal, microwave popcorn and, reluctantly, a couple of apples.

"Are you stalking me?"

Nate glanced over. It was the blonde from the restaurant.

"Uh, no," he said, flustered for a moment before he realized she'd been kidding.

She walked over to him, holding a shopping basket that contained actual vegetables.

"We saw each other last night," she said.

"I remember. How are you?"

"I'm good. Very good." She smiled, though Nate couldn't help but notice the sadness in her eyes. "I'm Alice."

"Hi, Alice. I'm Nate."

"Very pleased to meet you, Nate. Wow, what are the odds, huh? Do you shop here often?"

"I usually wait until I start thinking about how I can turn the baking soda into a meal."

"I buy one day's worth of food per trip, so I'm here all the time. I'm surprised we haven't run into each other before. Although we probably have and just didn't notice."

"So you live around here?" Nate asked.

"Not that close. But I'm picky about where I buy my food."

"I come here because it's the closest one. I always thought it was a pretty mediocre store, to be honest."

"They have good veggies."

"Gotcha. Not my area of expertise."

"How'd your date go?"

"How did you know it was a date?"

"You weren't at ease."

"It sucked," said Nate. "I mean, it really, truly sucked. You don't have to be a ray of sunshine all the time, but there's a point where you're physically draining happiness away from the people around you. Like, she may have permanently diminished my capacity for joy, like when a laptop battery stops charging all the way."

"That's really unfortunate. I would've come over and rescued you if I'd known."

"I tried to signal you. You didn't see the pleading in my eyes?"

"I was too far away," said Alice. "I apologize."

"Apology accepted. Just know that I'm a hollow shell of a man, if you can even call me a man anymore. You could have done something to prevent that."

"I'll make it up to you. How about I buy you lunch?"

"Seriously?"

Alice nodded. "I'll buy you a really great burger and see if we can get you up to ninety-one percent joy capacity."

"You don't have to do that. I accept your invitation, but we'll do separate checks."

"All right. However you want to do it." She jiggled her basket. "I'm just about done, but these frozen peas can't stay in the hot car. Should we finish shopping, take our stuff home, and meet in an hour?"

"That would be great."

"Have you ever been to Grizzle's?"

"No," said Nate.

"Oh, their food is delicious. The biggest, greasiest burgers you can imagine. Anything you'd be ashamed to admit you put on a burger is on their list of toppings. They should call the place Shame Burger. After I go there it's nothing but celery sticks for a week, but it's totally worth it."

"You have fully captured my attention."

"Do you need the address?"

"Is there more than one location?"

"Nope."

"Then I'll just use my GPS."

"Perfect. I'll see you there." She winked at him and walked away.

That was...weird.

Catching a woman's eye while on a terrible blind date, then

happening to run into her at the grocery store the next day, then having her ask you out—that was something out of a romantic comedy, not real life.

But, hey, Nate enjoyed a good romantic comedy.

He finished shopping and drove home. After putting away the groceries, he decided that a shower, a shave, and changing into clothes that he got out of the dresser instead of off the floor was a good idea. She'd asked him out to lunch when he was unshaven and his hair was sticking up in the back, so maybe she liked scruffy guys, but he didn't want her to smell body odor over the burger grease.

WHEN HE ARRIVED, ALICE WAS ALREADY SEATED AT A BOOTH IN THE back. She too had changed into different, nicer clothes. She waved him over, and he sat down across from her.

"I'm glad you actually came," she said.

"Why wouldn't I?"

"I don't know. It's not the most normal way to end up having lunch with somebody you just met. I wouldn't blame you if you got creeped out and bailed."

"It's okay," said Nate. "I brought my pepper spray."

"Smart."

"I like your necklace," said Nate. It was a strange silver eyeball necklace. He wasn't really one to notice jewelry, but it was pretty cool.

"Oh, thank you."

Nate opened the menu. "So what's the best burger they've got here?"

"The Big Grizzle. If you can eat the whole thing in forty-five minutes, it's free."

"Yeah, that's not how I'm looking to impress you right now."

"A lot of the specialty burgers are good, but I usually just get the one-third pounder and customize the toppings."

After studying the menu, Nate concluded that maybe Alice didn't need to witness him scarfing down a burger that could cause an immediate cardiac arrest. He went with a standard bacon cheeseburger. Alice ordered the same thing. They decided to split an order of fries, which was more intimate than Nate usually got when having lunch with somebody for the first time.

"So, what do you do?" Nate asked.

"In my spare time, or...?"

"As a job."

"Computer stuff. Boring. Very boring. And you?"

"I'm a restaurant server."

"Oh. That sounds interesting."

Nate smiled. "No, it doesn't, and you know it."

Alice took a drink of water. "Well, we haven't known each other long enough for me to make fun of your career choice."

"It wasn't a choice."

"How long have you been doing it?"

"Four years."

"Sounds like it might be a choice."

"Maybe."

Alice frowned. "I'm sorry. I was just trying to be funny. I didn't mean to offend you."

"No, no, you didn't offend me."

"I did. I'm so sorry. I talk without thinking sometimes. Please don't be mad."

"I'm not mad, and you didn't offend me."

"You promise?"

"I promise."

She took another drink of water. "Okay. What would be your dream career?"

"Playwright."

"Oh, that's cool. I love live theater. Are you working on anything now?"

"Uh-huh."

"Will you tell me about it?"

To Nate's surprise, he was happy to. He carefully watched her face for signs that she was just being polite, but she seemed genuinely interested in his tale of mistaken identity and redemption. She laughed at all the funny lines he shared, asked questions, and made a couple of suggestions that he'd definitely incorporate into his ongoing rewrite.

He didn't like to talk about his works in progress. Hated it. He wasn't sure if he felt bizarrely comfortable around Alice, or if maybe he felt like the stakes were low because he'd just met her, and it wouldn't matter much if she said, "Wow, that sounds like total dogshit."

Their burgers arrived partway through his description, and Nate's was indeed as delicious as Alice had promised. Alice only took a few small bites of hers, and also left most of her share of the fries uneaten, but Nate didn't get the impression she asked strangers out to lunch on a regular basis. She was probably nervous.

"What about you?" Nate asked. "Any kids?"

A flash of sadness. "No."

"Pets?"

"I'm between pets right now."

"Hobbies?"

"I love to play the piano, but I'm awful at it. I'm really terrible. I practice, but I never improve. When I sing along it's even worse. But I live alone, and I don't share walls with anyone, so there are no innocent victims."

"I'd like to hear you play sometime," said Nate.

"No, you wouldn't. Trust me on this. This isn't false humility. I'm not understating my abilities so that it's a big surprise when you discover that I'm a musical genius. The sounds I make...they're not good sounds. It's not pleasing to the ear. No, just no."

"All right. If I see you in the same room as a piano, I'll take offensive action."

The server walked over to the table asked if they needed anything else. "Oh, no, I'm stuffed," Alice told him. "Thank you."

"One check or separate?"

Alice looked over at Nate. "Last chance."

"Separate," Nate told the server. To Alice, he said, "It's very nice of you to offer, but it's not necessary." He briefly wondered if he should be paying for her meal; but no, she'd asked him out, and separate checks was fair.

The server left. Alice wiped her mouth off with her napkin. "Well, this was a lot of fun. Thanks for being my lunch date."

"Thanks for inviting me."

"You know, I have nowhere else to be for a while."

"Unfortunately, I do," said Nate. "I have to be at work by three."

"Oh, okay, of course. What time do you get off?"

"Eleven."

"I'll still be up at eleven." Alice's face fell. "Wow, I just sounded really desperate there, didn't I?"

"Nah, it's fine."

"That's the kind of woman who shows up unannounced at the place you work, or has a meltdown because she sees you having lunch with your sister. That's not me. I promise."

"I'd love to see you again at eleven, if you don't mind me smelling like fajitas."

Alice shook her head. "No, no, no, I don't want you to hear

horror movie music in your mind when you see me. Here's what we're going to do. I'm going to give you my phone number, but you're not going to give me yours. If you choose to call me, tomorrow or some other time in the future, the ball is in your court. If you choose not to, no harm, no foul, I enjoyed our brief time together, and I'm fine to leave it at that. I want you to have free will until we get married." She grimaced. "That was a joke. A scary joke. I'm sorry."

"I'll give you my phone number."

"I don't want it."

"It's okay, really."

"No, I made a stalker-sounding comment, and I don't want you worrying that I'm going to be hiding in your closet." She furrowed her brow. "I feel like I'm not improving things."

"Fine. I won't give you my phone number. All I'm going to say is that if I'd asked *you* what time you got off work and told you that I was available at eleven o'clock, I wouldn't feel like I'd made a scary stalker dude comment. You didn't even give me a teeny-tiny heart palpitation."

"That's very sweet."

"I don't think we've even told each other our last names," said Nate.

"Vinestalk. Alice Vinestalk. It sounds like a made-up last name, but I swear it isn't."

"Nate Sommer."

"A pleasure to meet you, Nate Sommer."

"A pleasure to meet you, Ms. Vinestalk. But I've gotta get going."

"Okay. I'll see you later. Or not."

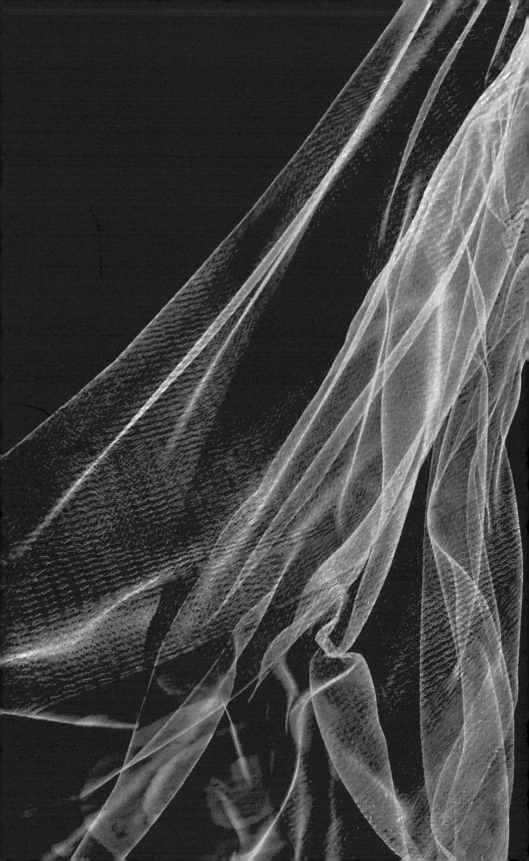

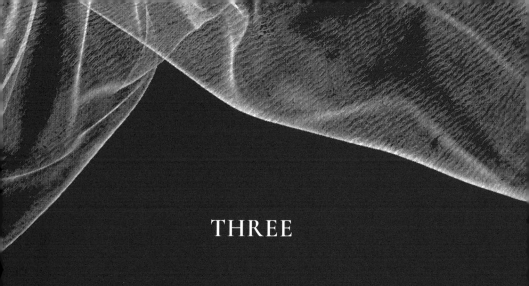

THREE

Nate was definitely going to call her back.

Yes, she was a little odd—he'd go with "quirky." But he liked odd/quirky. Obviously, there was a big red line in the air with "quirky" on one side and "frightening" on the other, but he didn't think she had come close to crossing that line yet. He'd enjoyed lunch. Though he wasn't getting a soulmate vibe from her, he wanted to hang out with her again. See where it went.

Josh, who was four hours into his own shift when Nate arrived, walked over to him as he punched in. "How come you never told me you were gay?"

"Never seemed important."

"Now you've complicated things. Chet was my closest gay friend. What am I supposed to tell him?"

"I'm playing along," said Nate, "but I have no idea what you're talking about."

"Gretchen is telling everybody you're gay. Not the specific word she's using, but that's the basic gist."

"Gotcha. How did things go with Stacey?"

"I licked her ice cream cone."

"Is that innuendo?"

"No. Literal. I got black cherry, and she got chocolate, and she let me taste hers."

"So you licked the ice cream, not the cone," said Nate. "Licking the actual cone would be weird."

"I was trying to make it sound like innuendo."

"You did a terrible job."

Craig, their manager, came into the back room to inform Nate and Josh that he did not pay them to sit around and chat. Armed with this newfound information, they went out to provide service to restaurant customers.

Throughout the rest of Josh's shift, they updated each other on their respective situations. Josh told Nate that he and Stacey made out for a while, which Nate thought was great, and Nate told Josh all about his experience with Alice, which Josh thought was insane.

After getting off work, Nate considered texting Alice but decided against it. By the time he got home and took a shower, it would be nearly midnight, and midnight texts fell squarely into booty call territory.

The next morning, after two bowls of cereal, he texted the number she'd given him. *Hi. It's Nate.*

Seconds later: *Hi, Nate!*

How's it going?

Can u call? Slow thumbs.

Sure.

"Thanks for calling me," Alice said. "I was hoping you would."

"Like I said, I really enjoyed talking to you yesterday. I don't know what your work schedule's like today, but I don't go in until three again, so I was checking to see if you were available to do lunch—this time my treat."

"I work from home and set my own hours."

"Ooooh, that's nice. I'm jealous."

"I'm not gonna lie. It's great."

"Kind of hard to make that work as a waiter. Customers usually aren't willing to make the trip to your house."

"Plus, you can't work in your pajamas," said Alice.

"You get to work in your pajamas?"

"Hell yeah."

"What's it like? Tell me all about it. Slowly."

Alice laughed. "Maybe you'll sell a play for big bucks, and then you too can work in your PJ's."

"Maybe. Not burning my other clothes yet."

"Or you'll find a patron to support you while you create your art."

"That's a great idea," said Nate. "Brilliant. I can totally get behind that. You're rich, right?"

"I wish."

"Would you be willing to take on a second job to give me and my muse a life of luxury?"

"Do I have to decide right away?"

"Nope. So, lunch?"

"Yes, absolutely," said Alice.

"Any preference on where to go?"

"Do you like fresh air and exercise?"

"In small amounts."

"There's a park I love. Lots of beautiful trails. I'll make us some sandwiches, and we can go for a hike."

"That sounds like fun," said Nate. "But I invited you, so I'll make the sandwiches."

"I saw your grocery cart. You don't have sandwich materials."

"I didn't see any bread in your basket."

"But you hate to shop, and I don't."

"That is true."

"How does eleven-thirty sound? We won't take the long trails. I'll get you to work on time."

"Okay."

"Meet at the park? I pick you up? You pick me up?"

"I'll pick you up."

"Don't want me to know where you live?" asked Alice. "Kidding."

"I was just trying to make it easier for you," said Nate.

"What kind of sandwich do you want?"

"Anything's fine."

"But what kind is your favorite?"

"Let's go with turkey."

"Turkey Swiss?"

"Sure."

"I'll text you my address. Eleven-thirty."

She didn't live all that close to him—Nate had to leave at a quarter to eleven to be there by eleven-thirty. He pulled into the driveway of a small, one-story light-blue home in a neighborhood that seemed okay during the day but probably wasn't somewhere you'd walk at night without a large, vicious dog to accompany you.

Alice came outside, beaming as she saw him. She was carrying a brown grocery bag. She got into the passenger seat of his car, shut the door, fastened her seat belt, and held up the bag. "Turkey Swiss sandwiches. I made one on white and one on rye, so you can choose. I've got one bag of corn chips and one bag of potato chips. I brought bottled water, but they have a vending machine at the park by the restrooms if you want a can of soda."

"You seem very prepared."

"Just want it to be fun."

"I'm sure it will be."

IT WAS.

Nature hikes were not Nate's first choice for an afternoon of recreation, but he was in good physical shape, and he wasn't gasping for breath and pleading with Alice to slow down. The weather was perfect. The scenery was beautiful, if a bit repetitious.

Nate was not a big "long-term relationship" guy. His longest so far had been just under a year. (Admittedly, she'd broken up with him, so, in theory, they could've still been together if he'd been calling the shots.) He didn't consider himself commitment-phobic; he simply found that his relationships were more enjoyable if they were over relatively soon.

Although he'd had a lot of short-term monogamous girlfriends, he'd never met anybody with whom he had as much in common as with Alice. They both loved science fiction novels and movies. She'd lost a parent at a young age; her mother to cancer, while he'd lost his father to a heart attack. Her loss at age twelve, his at fourteen. Three of their five favorite television shows overlapped. If nothing romantic came out of this, he was sure they could at least be friends. He simply enjoyed her company.

Admittedly, despite her upbeat demeanor, there was an undeniable underlying sadness. Her smile didn't always reach her eyes. She gave the impression of a woman putting on a brave front. Had she been abused? Was she still coping with a tragic loss? Was it a deep loneliness that lunch and a hike with Nate wasn't enough to overcome?

He kept quiet about it, letting her play the role of the happy-go-lucky woman. If they continued to see each other, she'd eventually tell him.

But hey, the turkey Swiss sandwich (he picked the one on rye) was delicious.

After a couple of hours in the park, they returned to his car. The conversation on the drive home was devoted to how much their musical tastes were in sync. When he pulled into Alice's driveway, she unfastened her seat belt but didn't open the door.

"Thank you," she said. "This was a lot of fun. Again."

"Do you want to get together tomorrow?"

"I'd love that."

"Great."

She looked at him, and her face turned very serious. "You can kiss me if you want. You don't have to—I'm not trying to force you —but if you want to, you can."

He kissed her.

As he pulled away, she smiled. "You're a good kisser."

"So are you."

"We'll kiss some more tomorrow."

"I look forward to it."

"I'd say that we should've gone longer and sloppier, but you don't have tinted windows, and I have neighbors."

"Next time," said Nate.

"Next time for sure. See you soon." She got out of the car, waved, and walked to her front door. She peeked back at him and grinned as she unlocked the door and went inside.

Nate drove off. He wasn't in love, and he wasn't infatuated, but he really liked her. She was intriguing, and even if he never discovered the origin story that made her hurt inside, he enjoyed being around her. They certainly didn't need to get together every single day, but he was looking forward to tomorrow.

THE NEXT DAY HIS SHIFT STARTED WHEN THE RESTAURANT OPENED, so he punched out at six-thirty. During the day, he'd found himself curiously not wanting to share details with Josh, even though there was nothing remotely scandalous to report. Josh and Stacey had decided to take a break, which seemed odd since they'd only been together for a couple of days and hadn't slept together yet, but Josh assured him that everything was fine and, besides, he'd hooked up with Gretchen.

Alice invited Nate over to watch a couple of movies. "Your choice," she'd explained. He picked up a pizza on the way, along with a bouquet of flowers.

Her eyes lit up as she opened the door. "Oh, that's so nice of you!" She took the flowers from him and inhaled deeply. "Thank you. That's very romantic."

She led him inside, assuring him that he didn't have to take off his shoes first. "There's not much to see, but here's the grand tour," she said, taking him from room to room.

Nate would've expected clutter. Shelves overflowing with books arranged in no particular order. Paintings on the walls that made you stop, go "Huh?" and take a closer look. A collection of dolls that you wouldn't want to turn your back on.

Instead, the house was mostly non-descript. No paintings or pictures on the walls. Sparse furniture. None of the little touches that made a house a home. It had the feeling that she'd just moved there and had yet to finish unpacking.

"How long have you lived here?" Nate asked, as she led him down a hallway.

"About a year."

"Do you really drive this far to the grocery every day? That's over an hour round-trip."

Alice stopped walking. She didn't turn around to face him.

"Yeah, about that," she said.

"I didn't mean anything by it."

"I...okay, Nate, I should tell you something." Now she turned around. She looked like her skin was suddenly very itchy. "Sometimes I just say things. I don't lie—I mean, I don't consciously lie, but things come out of my mouth and I think, 'Why the hell did you say that?' but it's too late to take them back."

"Okay," said Nate. He didn't actually take a step away from her, but he was tempted to do so.

"The store by you isn't where I normally shop. I was on that side of town for a doctor's appointment, and I decided I might as well pick up some things since the store was right there. Save me a trip to my usual grocery. Then I saw you and remembered you from the previous night, and it just seemed weird that we happened to see each other twice so close together. Then my idiot mouth took over and tried to make it seem like less of a coincidence, even though coincidences like that happen all the time. I don't know. I guess I just didn't want you to think I'd planned it or something. Now I have to confess everything, and I'm coming off way worse than if I'd just told the truth in the first place. I hate my brain. I'm sorry."

She stopped talking. Nate felt like he should say something, but wasn't sure what he had to contribute to the conversation at that moment.

"You can leave," she told him. "I'd understand. You won't hurt my feelings."

"I don't want to leave."

"I don't want you to leave, either, but I'm very awkward, and I'm going to continue to be awkward, and this will happen again."

"It's really okay," he assured her. It wasn't *completely* okay, and he couldn't deny that he was feeling more than a little wary. Yet he hadn't shown up with pizza thinking he was going to spend the evening with the most normal, well-adjusted woman in the world.

It was a big-ass red flag, but he wouldn't flee quite yet.

"I'll make you a deal," he said. "Neither of us will mention it again. I won't mention it, you won't mention it, and we'll pretend it never happened. It'll be a collective gap in our memories."

"I'd like that," said Alice.

"Good. Let's eat pizza and watch movies."

Nate couldn't make it into an actual gap in his memory.

It was just a bit too strange for him to completely let go. But he would stick to his vow not to mention it again, not even to Josh. (*Especially* not to Josh, who would say, "Run, dude, run!")

Alice had asked him what he wanted to watch. He said it was her choice. She started to say something back, but he could tell that she decided that she should stop being overly accommodating, and she picked *Galaxy Quest*, one of his favorites. They sat on her couch, ate pepperoni pizza, and watched the movie without talking, though there was plenty of laughter.

"I haven't seen that since I was a kid," said Alice, as the credits rolled. "I'd forgotten how good it was."

"Oh, yeah. I love everything about it."

"It's gonna be hard to top that choice."

"Yep."

She stared at him for a long moment. "May I be really blunt with you? I mean, almost cartoonishly blunt?"

"Sure."

Alice hesitated, as if working up the courage to speak. "I'd like to watch a second movie, but I think our time would be better spent if you sat there on the couch and I went down on you."

Nate had no immediate response to that.

After about ten seconds, he decided that he should probably react. "You were right," he said. "That was very blunt."

"No pressure," she said with a nervous giggle.

"No pressure felt."

They were silent for another ten seconds.

"I mean, yeah, okay," he said. "That would be nice, if that's what you wanted to do."

"It may not top *Galaxy Quest*, but I'll give it my best shot."

FOUR

"Do you want to take off your pants, or do you want me to do it?" Alice asked.

"Um, whatever, I'm good either way, you can do it."

Alice got up off the couch, turned off the light, then crouched down in front of him. She unbuttoned his jeans.

Nate had a couple of condoms in his wallet, so it would be disingenuous for him to suggest that he never, ever imagined that such a thing was possible. Asked to place a wager on whether the evening would have gone in this direction, he would've bet on: *not entirely out of the realm of possibility, but most likely not this time.* He knew it *could* happen, but he was taken aback that it *was* happening.

She could just be messing with him, although she'd now unzipped his pants, making the idea that it was a ruse much less likely.

"Lift up," she said. Nate lifted up enough for her to tug his jeans down to his knees. He'd worn one of his nicest pairs of boxer shorts; again, he hadn't anticipated that he'd be in this position, but still, better to be prepared than not.

She gently ran her hand over his crotch. He was already responding.

"If I'm doing anything wrong, or if there's something you'd like me to do differently, don't hesitate to let me know," she said.

"I'm sure I won't need to do that."

"But if you *want* to, please speak up. Communication is important. I want you to be completely satisfied."

"Gotcha," said Nate. Now he was genuinely wondering if this was a joke. Maybe she had a webcam hidden somewhere, and he was about to star in an uproariously funny livestream about guys who mistakenly believe they're about to get a blowjob.

"It doesn't have to be the best oral sex you've ever had," she said. "I just want to make sure it's really good."

"I'm sure it will be great," Nate assured her. He almost said, "I'll fill out a comment card afterward," and decided that though she'd *probably* think it was funny, the small chance that she wouldn't meant he should keep the comment safely locked away in his brain.

"Lift up again."

Nate lifted up, and she pulled his boxers down to his knees. She leaned forward and took him into her mouth.

Okay. If it was a prank, she was taking it pretty far.

Maybe it was revenge. Maybe she was representing somebody he'd wronged in the past, and very soon her teeth would come into play.

Nah. Nate wasn't universally beloved, but to the best of his knowledge, he hadn't made any enemies who hated him enough to go to this length for vengeance.

He closed his eyes and tried to just lose himself in the pleasure.

He opened his eyes again, unable to lose himself in the pleasure.

She was making eye contact. She pulled her mouth away from him. "Am I doing it okay?"

Nate nodded. "Perfect."

"I'm sure it's not *perfect*."

"It is. Don't change a thing."

She resumed going down on him. Nate started to relax. Why did he think this was so weird? Plenty of guys had this happen on their third date. The third date was the sex date. This was the standard progression of adult relationships. There was nothing bizarre about what was happening right now.

Alice being socially awkward didn't mean she couldn't be horny.

Nate gave in to the experience. Alice didn't speak anymore, and Nate communicated only through moans. A few minutes later, he'd reached that moment where it was important to be considerate. "I'm gonna come," he gasped.

She nodded without pulling her mouth away, made direct eye contact, and picked up the pace.

Nate didn't try to hold back. He finished with a loud groan.

Alice swallowed and wiped her lips with her index finger. "Good?" she asked.

"Oh, God, yes." He took a moment to catch his breath. "Your turn."

"Oh, no, I'm okay."

"You sure?"

"Yep. This was about *you*."

"Okay," said Nate. "Let me know if you change your mind."

"I will." Alice stood up and smoothed out her shirt. She smiled at him. "We still have time for a second movie."

THEY DIDN'T GET VERY FAR INTO THE SECOND MOVIE BEFORE THEY started making out. This was no reflection on the quality of the filmmaking—it was simply that they couldn't keep their hands or lips off each other. Alice kept her clothes on, but allowed him to do a generous amount of groping.

Eventually they stopped and just snuggled for the last half hour. "Thank you for a wonderful evening," said Alice, as the credits rolled. "I hope we can do a lot more of this."

"Definitely."

"Sometime soon I'll ask you to spend the night. Not quite yet, though."

"I completely understand."

She led him to her front door and sent him away with a tight hug and a gentle kiss on the lips.

Nate drove home feeling great. He was never good at figuring out the moment when somebody officially became a girlfriend, and he was pretty sure they weren't there yet, but he looked forward to spending more time with her.

He was really wired when he walked into his apartment, so he popped open a can of beer, turned on some music, and decided to play around online for a bit. Might as well follow Alice on social media. She was pretty easy to find—"Alice Vinestalk" wasn't exactly a common name—and after he sent a friend request he casually scrolled through her Facebook feed. She didn't post very often. Mostly food pics and selfies. Her relationship status was "Divorced" but no other details. Twitter and Instagram were about the same. She had a TikTok account but, disappointingly, hadn't posted any videos.

His phone buzzed. A text from Alice read: *Had a great time tonight.*

Me too! Just sent you a Facebook friend request.

Ugh, I hate social media LOL. But I'll accept.

A moment later, Nate got a notification that she'd accepted the request.

Shortly after that, he got a notification that she had requested to change her status to "In a relationship" with him.

Screw it. Why not? They *were* in a relationship. He clicked "approve."

We're Facebook official! Alice texted. *Can I give you a quick call to say goodnight?*

Of course!

It wasn't a quick call. They talked late into the night.

HE WOKE UP TO A TEXT FROM HER: *CONGRATULATIONS! I'M GIVING you the day off from me! Enjoy this breather, because I'm going to wear your ass out tomorrow.*

I have the day off tomorrow. Should I rent a defibrillator?

Wouldn't hurt.

"HOW ARE THINGS GOING WITH THE SCARY CHICK?" JOSH ASKED AS soon as Nate arrived at the restaurant.

"She's not scary."

"Did she make you say that at knifepoint?"

"Seriously, she's great. You'd like her."

"Until she serves me my dog in a casserole."

"*Enough,*" said Nate. "Stop being a dick."

Josh blinked with surprise. "Whoa, what's your deal?"

"My deal is that you're being an asshole. Leave her alone."

"Dude, I didn't mean anything by it. This is the way we talk to each other. Sorry for not getting the memo that our entire social dynamic has changed."

"You're right, you're right," said Nate. "I overreacted. Things are going great with Alice."

"Is it super serious?"

Nate shrugged. "I'm not saying that. I'm just saying that I really like her."

"All right," said Josh. "Fair enough. I'll stop making jokes about her being scary."

"Thanks. How are things with Gretchen?"

"Overall, pretty bad, but the hate-fucking is incredible."

Want to come over? Alice texted the next day.

I sure as hell do!

Can't wait! Bring your laptop.

She greeted him at the door with a kiss. "Here's my proposal," she said. "I think you should work on your play all day."

"Oh, okay," said Nate, a bit confused.

"And we should have a rewards system. When you reach certain progress goals, you get...*favors*. You know what I mean."

"I am one hundred percent for that."

"If you had a really good day, how many pages would you write?"

"It depends. I'm actually done with the first draft of the play, but it's kind of a mess. There are some scenes that I skipped, so I guess I could write those."

"How many pages' worth of missing scenes are there?" asked Alice.

"Ten, maybe?"

"So I could reward you for every page you wrote?"

Nate nodded. "Although I'd probably pick up where I left off with the rewrite, and just add the new material as I went along." Why the hell was he overcomplicating this?

"How many pages is the whole thing?"

"Ninety-two now, so it'll be around a hundred, hundred and two when I'm done."

"I'm not giving you a hundred and two blowjobs."

"That's understandable."

"I guess I could reward you for units of time spent working on it, but that kind of defeats the purpose," said Alice. "You could be rewarded for just staring at your screen."

"I'm making this too convoluted," said Nate. "Let's stick with a favor for each new page of material."

"Well, I don't want you to mess up your normal process. Maybe you could get rewarded for every ten pages of rewrites and for every page of new material."

"That works."

"But then how do I know you actually did any revision? You might have just fixed a typo or two. I think you need to send me the play, and I'll compare the revised version to the original and decide if you've earned the sexual favor."

"I...I, uh, don't like people reading my stuff before it's done. I didn't mind telling you about it, but I'd rather not have you actually read it until I'm happy with it."

"We're not making this easy," said Alice.

"Sorry."

"Okay. We're going to go with an honor system here. You're going to sit and work on your play all day, and whenever you feel you've earned a sexual favor, I'll grant it. But if I feel like you're scamming me, there'll be punishment."

"What kind of punishment?"

Alice smiled. "You don't want to know."

"That sounds fair."

"I don't have a desk. Do you want to write on the couch, or on the kitchen table?"

"I was hoping to write in a bubble bath."

"Then you'll be very disappointed."

"The couch is fine," said Nate. "What are you going to do while I'm working?"

"Hover over you and stare."

"Sounds creepy."

"I was kidding."

"I know. 'Sounds creepy' was also kidding."

"I'm going to stand here with a cattle prod, ready to zap you if you go too long without typing anything. And I'm not kidding. Except the part about the cattle prod. I was kidding about that."

There was something just a bit off about Alice's delivery, like she was trying too hard to engage in banter. He wondered what her romantic history was like.

"How long were you married?" he asked.

Why the hell had he just blurted it out like that? Where was the natural transition to another subject? Clearly, Alice wasn't the only one who was socially awkward.

Alice narrowed her eyes. "Why?"

"I didn't mean that in an accusing way or anything. It came out completely wrong. Your Facebook page said you were divorced, and I was curious."

"Six years. Most of them weren't happy."

"Okay. Seriously, I wasn't asking it like I was trying to say that you should have told me already. I was just wondering about your dating history."

"Wondering if I've offered sexual favors to other guys in exchange for expressing themselves creatively?"

Nate shook his head. "No. That wasn't it at all."

"I've had sex with four men. My boyfriend in college. My husband right out of college. A long dry spell. A terrible one-night stand. And then you. If you don't count because it was just oral, then I've had sex with three men."

"I think I should count."

"So, no, I haven't offered sexual favors to other guys for writing."

"I never asked that," said Nate. Shit. He was ruining this. He'd been presented with this complete fantasy experience, and he might have screwed it up. He had to tread very carefully if he wanted to salvage this. "My timing was all off. I'm sorry."

"It's okay," said Alice, though it wasn't clear from her tone if the day's planned activities were still going to happen.

"I'll be honest. No woman has ever offered to do something like this for me. My head is spinning. I'm not the kind of guy who can play it cool and think, 'Yeah, this happens all the time.' It doesn't. Ever."

"You'd never had a blowjob before me?"

"Yes, I'd had blowjobs. What I meant was—"

"I was kidding again," said Alice. "We're fine."

"You sure?"

"I'm sure. I assume you want caffeine while you write, so I've got coffee and Red Bull."

"Coffee would be great."

"Cream and sugar?"

"Lots of both."

"All right. Get comfy. You've got a ton of work to do today."

IT WAS THE MOST PRODUCTIVE WRITING DAY OF NATE'S LIFE.

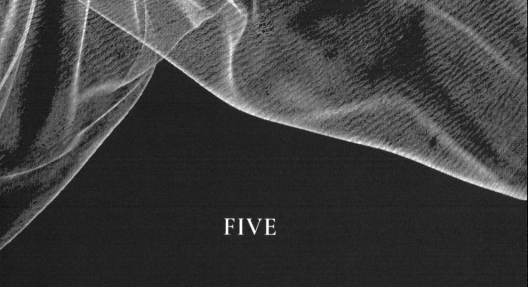

FIVE

*S*he let him spend the night.

The rewards system—and no, Nate did not cheat even once—had been fun and lighthearted. Lots of pleasurable teasing. A clumsy but enthusiastic lap dance. Plenty of licks. She did not stare creepily at him while he worked, but rather sat on the other end of the couch, reading a hardcover fantasy novel.

When he admitted that he'd hit the wall on his play, Alice took him by the hand and led him to her bedroom.

"I'm not ready to go all the way," she said. "I want to save that. But there's plenty else we can do."

They turned out the lights, climbed into bed, and did a great many things. They fell asleep for a couple of hours afterward, then awoke, famished. Nate raided her cupboard, then prepared his specialty: macaroni and cheese out of a box.

"What next?" Alice asked, when they were finished eating. "Want to watch a movie?"

"Do you have any board games?"

Alice shook her head. "Well, I do, I have Monopoly and Yahtzee, I think, but games don't sound fun right now."

"Not even Truth or Dare?"

"No way. You writers lie for a living."

"I *wish* I could lie for a living," said Nate.

"Someday you will. And I'll be encouraging you every step of the way."

They decided to snuggle on the couch and watch a movie. But the movie sucked, so after about twenty minutes she led him back into the bedroom, where they eventually fell asleep in each other's arms. Normally, Nate would cuddle for as long as required and then move to the other side of the bed so that his appendages wouldn't fall asleep, but he and Alice seemed to fit together perfectly, and he didn't wake up until the next morning.

In the morning, Alice slid out of bed and walked toward the bathroom.

Nate whistled. "Nice ass, lady!"

She looked over her shoulder at him, smiled, and gave it a little wiggle. "Thank you."

"One more kiss."

She hesitated, then turned around and walked back to the bed.

Nate couldn't help but look at her C-section scar. Then he quickly looked away, as if she'd caught him staring.

Alice traced the scar with her index finger. "Gross, huh?"

Nate vigorously shook his head. "You can barely see it. And even if you could, it's not gross."

"Thanks." Alice sighed. "I know you have a legitimate question about this, but is it okay if we don't talk about it now? We can if you want. It just really hurts, and it's...it's a conversation for another time."

"Of course. We can talk about it whenever you're ready, or not at all. It's totally up to you."

She gave him a kiss. "That means a lot to me."

Alice went into the bathroom and closed the door. God. No wonder he noticed an undercurrent of sadness in her. She'd probably lost a child. He wasn't going to push for the story, but he'd hold her tight when she was finally ready to tell it.

After they got dressed, he made her breakfast. There was a reason he was a restaurant server and not a chef, but he could make decent French toast, and Alice seemed to have no complaints. They bid each other farewell with a kiss, and Nate returned home until his shift began.

He definitely had a girlfriend now. And he liked it.

THE NEXT WEEK WAS ABSOLUTELY FREAKING AWESOME.

They got along great. He quickly became used to Alice's awkwardness, and there were no further tense exchanges. They slept together every night, alternating between her place and his. It had taken a few days for her to go all the way with him, but Nate was plenty satisfied before that, and the experience of being inside her surpassed all expectations.

Nate finished another draft of *Frank, Frank, & Frank*. He made Alice read it in another room, because it made him too nervous to watch her as she read, though he did listen carefully for the sounds of laughter. She proclaimed it to be a masterpiece, and he didn't detect any signs that she was full of shit. After heaping lavish praise upon his work, she offered some constructive criticism that was completely on-point.

Meanwhile, Josh had gotten back together with Shelly, who did not know that he'd hooked up with Gretchen, and Nate and Alice had a double date with them that went extremely well. Josh admitted later that, yes, Alice was kind of weird, but he really liked her and was happy for Nate.

After the double date, Nate and Alice lay in her bed, her head on his chest. Nate was just about to fall asleep when Alice spoke. "Do you promise not to freak out if I tell you something?" she asked.

"Maybe."

"I won't say it, then."

"No, no, it's fine," said Nate. "I assume you're not going to confess to murder."

"Nothing like that."

"Let's hear it."

"I shouldn't have said anything."

"I promise I won't freak out."

"Actually, you can freak out. It's okay. I'm a big girl. I can handle it."

"All right," said Nate, who was becoming very nervous about what she was going to say. They'd used protection, but that didn't mean she wasn't about to tell him she was pregnant.

"I'm not pregnant," she said.

"I didn't think you were."

"You looked really worried, and I thought that's where your mind was going."

"Nah. I mean, a little."

"I wouldn't force you to raise the baby with me if I was."

"Well, I wouldn't think of you as *forcing* me."

"I'm not here to ruin your life, Nate. If I was pregnant, which I'm not, I promise, I'd like for us to raise the baby together, but I wouldn't trap you into anything. Not even child support."

"I'd—" Nate started to assure her that he'd pay child support, but it was very strange to be having this kind of conversation about a child who had not been conceived. Telling her he'd pay for child support was as strange as her telling him he wouldn't have to. "I feel like we're getting sidetracked."

"Yeah," said Alice. She gave him several gentle kisses on his chest.

"So what did you want to tell me?"

"It's not important."

"If you don't tell me, I'll assume the worst. Like you've developed a taste for human flesh, and you kept waking up wondering how you'd cook me."

"Oh, I wouldn't cook you, sweetheart. I'd eat you raw." Alice grinned, but again, it seemed a bit forced, like she was trying too hard to be playful.

"You're not going to tell me, are you?"

"What do you *think* I was going to say?"

"I don't know."

"Think hard."

"I really don't know," Nate admitted.

She gazed directly into his eyes. "I love you."

"Oh," said Nate. A millisecond later, he recognized that "Oh" was a terrible response, and immediately followed it up with, "I love you, too."

Now her grin seemed genuine. Her entire face lit up. "Do you really?"

"Yes. I really do."

Did he? As with the "When is she officially my girlfriend?" question, the awareness of exactly when he was in love eluded Nate. But he certainly liked her a hell of a lot, and he didn't want to break up with her, and if he hadn't quite fallen in love with her yet, saying, "I love you, too," was a harmless little white lie.

Alice snuggled tighter against him. And then they made love.

"You seem happier," said Josh, as they enjoyed a rare slow moment at the restaurant. "I hate to admit it, but I think Alice is really good for you."

"I agree," said Nate.

"I hear you took the next step."

"What next step?"

"Saying 'I love you' to each other."

"How did you know that?"

"She told Stacey."

"I didn't realize she'd stayed in touch with Stacey."

Josh nodded. "Oh, yeah. They're good friends now."

"Well, that's cool." And it was indeed cool. His girlfriend and Josh's girlfriend *should* be friends. Everybody had gotten along great during their double date, and there was absolutely no reason the two women shouldn't have continued to talk afterward. It was just a bit odd that Alice had never mentioned it.

"So I hear you and Stacey are friends now," he told Alice. They sat across from each other at his dining room table, having pancakes for dinner.

She poured some more syrup on her stack. "Yep. She's great!"

Alice didn't seem the least bit defensive. Not that she should, he supposed. But considering how much time he and Alice had spent together over the past week, it surprised him that she hadn't mentioned anything. Especially that she and his best friend's girlfriend were close enough that she told Stacey about the whole "I love you" thing.

But there was a lot he didn't know about her. She was clearly uncomfortable sharing personal details, choosing to focus on more superficial conversations. She never talked about her friends, and, quite honestly, he'd just assumed that she didn't have many, if any. He was delighted that she and Stacey were getting along so well, and Nate would *never* be the kind of boyfriend who got jealous about time spent with her friends, male or female. It was just a little strange that she hadn't told him she had a confidant. That's all. No big deal.

"Josh is great, too," said Alice. "He and Stacey make a wonderful couple."

"Really? You're literally the only person who thinks that. And I'm including Josh and Stacey."

Alice shrugged. "I just get along with your friends, I guess. I bet you have really fun times at the restaurant."

"We have more fun when we're not at the restaurant. It's not really a party job."

"Either way, you're lucky. And I'm looking forward to meeting your mom someday."

"Maybe."

"I said someday, not soon. I know she's in Portland and you never really see her. Just because you don't get along with her doesn't mean I don't want to meet her. It'll help me understand you."

Nate smiled. "You don't understand me?"

"Understand you *better*."

"I think that's pretty much a lost cause."

"Nah," said Alice. "I'll figure you out."

"Am I a beguiling mystery?"

"Sort of."

"I always thought I was really shallow."

"You're not Kierkegaard, but you're not a caveman, either."

Nate wanted to make a Kierkegaard joke, but he didn't actually know much about the guy except that he was a deep thinker, and he didn't want to prove himself to be a dumbass.

Anyway, he wasn't the mysterious one. He was a single guy who worked at a Tex-Mex restaurant while harboring dreams of being a successful playwright. He had plenty of embarrassing moments in his past, but not much in the way of secrets.

"What about me are you trying to figure out?" he asked.

"Bits and pieces here and there."

"Ask any questions you want. I'm an open book."

"No, that would spoil the fun."

"Once you crack the code, I think you're going to be very disappointed. I'm way closer to a caveman than..." Shit. He didn't want to say the name because he was suddenly worried that he might mispronounce it, thus proving his own point. "Dr. K."

"He wasn't a doctor, but I get what you're trying to say. My original point was just that I like your friends, and I want to meet your family, and I love you even if you're more of a primate than a philosopher."

They ate their pancakes, then followed them up with ice cream.

THE NEXT DAY AT WORK WAS PARTICULARLY BRUTAL. ONE OF THE cooks was hung over and off his game, leading to a lot of angry customers who acted as if Nate had prepared their meal himself. He'd never apologized so many times in a single day. Josh had the day off, that lucky son of a bitch.

When Nate's shift ended, he drove to Alice's house, looking forward to a hot shower and a foot rub. She greeted him at the door with her cell phone to her ear.

"Well, you have to understand it from his perspective," she said into the phone, gesturing for Nate to come inside. "He's a guy. Guys do that sometimes. It's not like you've been together for years, or even weeks. Yes, I hear what you're saying. I'm not taking sides. Had you specifically told each other that you were in a committed relationship? You can't assume it—you have to say it. Look, I'm going to be blunt. If he's cheating on you this soon in the relationship, you're not meeting his needs. Sorry, but that's just the way I see it. That's fine. Let it all out. You're not the first person to call me that." Alice lowered the phone and shrugged. "She hung up on me."

"Who was that?" Nate asked.

"Stacey."

"It didn't sound good."

"She went over to Josh's house without texting him first. Gretchen was there."

"Ooops."

"Yeah."

Nate sighed. "I wish I could say I was completely shocked."

"She'll get over it. He may just want to protect his genitals for a while."

"Josh is a great guy in many ways, but he's not the most...*monogamous* person in the world. I was surprised to hear you tell her that she wasn't meeting his needs. His only needs were for her not to stop him from having sex with Gretchen."

"I lied," Alice admitted. "I did take sides. I took your side. And I'm not going to put you in a bad position by calling your best friend an asshole. Josh is your friend, not Stacey, and if I have to choose between the two, I'm choosing Josh."

"You don't have to."

"Of course I do. Stacey's the outsider."

"Still..."

Alice shook her head. "This isn't about them. This is about us.

Considering she dropped about fifty F-bombs in two minutes, I'm pretty sure Stacey has no intention of taking him back. And if they're not together, I have no reason to be friends with her."

"You can still be friends with her."

"I know I *can* be friends with her. But I don't want to be around somebody who's trashing your buddy, even if maybe he deserves it. Don't give it another thought. I'm going to block her number."

"All right. Tomorrow at work I'll yell at him for being an idiot."

Alice kissed him. "Just so you know, I'd never tie you down. I won't take away your freedom. As long as you were honest and didn't sneak around behind my back, if there was something you wanted, I wouldn't stop you."

Nate stared at her for a moment. "Are you talking about an open relationship?"

"Halfway. I have no interest in anybody else, so I would not partake, but if you were tempted, as long as you didn't rub it in my face afterward, I'd be okay with it. And that applies no matter how serious our relationship gets."

"That's...quite an offer."

"I'm quite a woman."

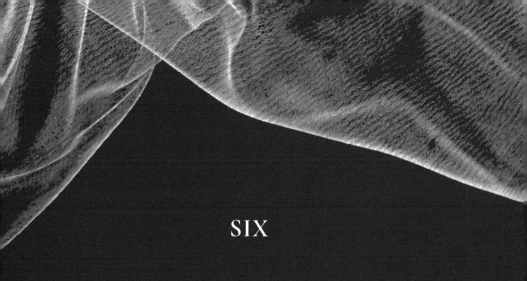

SIX

"Shit!" said Alice the next morning. She was on her work computer, while Nate sat on the other end of the couch, playing a word game on his phone, just hanging out until he had to leave for the restaurant. "Fuck!"

"What's wrong?"

"Nothing. Shit!"

"Sounds like it's *something*."

"It is," Alice admitted. "This sucks."

"What?"

"I knew it was a possibility, but I was hoping for the best." She let out a long, frustrated sigh. "I don't own this house. I rent. And the owner has decided to sell it."

"What does that mean for you?"

"It means that I have three weeks to find a new place to live. Shit!"

"Can the owner do that? Kick you out with so little notice?"

"Yeah, I was on a month-to-month lease. It was nice for me

because it gave me the flexibility to leave whenever I want, but, obviously, there's a downside."

"What are you going to do?" Nate asked.

"I don't know. Do you need a roomie?" She laughed. "I'm just kidding. Unless you do need a roomie."

"My apartment is pretty small."

"I've been in it. It's not so bad."

"It's the apartment of a restaurant server and aspiring playwright."

"Don't call yourself aspiring," said Alice. "You're a real play-wright. Don't diminish yourself like that."

"I'll never do it again."

"I'm not putting any pressure on you, I promise. And I know we haven't known each other very long. But we do practically live together already."

Nate didn't agree with that. Yes, they spent most of their free time together, and slept together every night, but that wasn't the same as cohabiting. The only items of hers at his apartment were her toothbrush and shampoo. The only item of Nate's at her house was his toothbrush—he used her shampoo when he was there.

They hadn't even exchanged spare keys yet. The "Should we move in together?" discussion should've been a long way off.

Alice noticed he looked very uncomfortable. She set her laptop on the coffee table, scooted closer to him, and placed her hand on his leg. "It's okay if you're not ready for it."

"It's not that I'm not ready for it," said Nate, not being entirely truthful. "There's a difference between spending time at each other's places, and actually sharing my apartment. I wouldn't have room for all your stuff."

"I'd put it in storage. You've got furniture and a TV and kitchen utensils and everything else we need. I'd bring a big bag of clothes, and that's basically it. And I wouldn't take up any of your closet space. I'd get one of those external wardrobe things—not a big heavy wooden one, but the one that's kind of like a rectangular tent. I'll show you what I mean later." She gestured around her living room. "And I'm tidy."

"I'm not."

"I know. I could be your housekeeper, unless you had a specific reason you wanted dirty socks on the floor."

"I mean...it might work," said Nate. "I wasn't really expecting to talk about this today."

"Neither was I. And to be clear, I lost my house, not my job. You're not taking in a stray. I'll pay half of the rent, buy my share of the groceries, cover utilities—all of that. And you don't have to add me to the lease. Not until you're ready. If it's not working, you can kick my ass right out, no questions asked."

"Has she sold the house already? You said she'd just decided to sell it."

"Right. She has to start getting it ready to sell."

"Okay." Nate wasn't sure what to say.

"You're being very quiet," said Alice.

"I'm sorry. This whole thing is moving at supersonic speed. It hasn't even been two weeks since we first met. It's been an amazing two weeks, but moving in together is a huge step."

Alice nodded. "It absolutely is. I would never have suggested it under normal circumstances."

"I need time to think about it."

"Of course, of course. As I said, I'm not trying to pressure you into anything. I'm getting kicked out of my house, and I have to move *somewhere*, so moving in with you was my first thought. But I completely understand if you're not ready for it. I'm not sure I'm ready for it, either. It just seemed like a quick and easy solution, since we're always at each other's places anyway. But it's totally fine if you say no. I won't be mad or hurt."

"I'm not saying no. I'm saying I want to think about it first."

"Good. You *should* think about it. I don't want you to think you made this decision without giving it proper consideration."

"Okay."

"But, again, I won't bring anything but the bare necessities. I'll pay half of everything. And you'll basically have a live-in sex slave. I'll do anything you want. Even if I don't like it."

"I don't want you to do things you don't like," said Nate.

"I would, though. For you. And maybe I'd learn to like them."

"That's not really a selling point. The sex slave part is, sure, but why would I want you to do things you don't enjoy? That's a weird pitch for moving in together."

"Well, I'm weird," said Alice. "You know that. And I apologize. I had an anxiety attack when I saw that I was getting kicked out of my house, then I got really excited when I thought we could be roomies, and I'm not sure why I decided to go with, 'We could do anal,' to plead my case. My brain confuses even me sometimes."

"It's all right."

"No, it's not all right. I need to learn how to handle a relation-ship without pushing the other person away."

"You're not pushing me away."

"Forget I brought it up."

"I never said no," Nate insisted. "This is a major life change, and I can't do it as a knee-jerk reaction. You don't know which way I'm leaning on this. My lease expires in three or four months. Maybe you should get a new place, something bigger than what I've got, and let me move in with you."

"For real?"

"Just brainstorming."

Nate wasn't sure why he'd said that. He was just trying to figure out how to keep from hurting her feelings. But it was insane to move in together this quickly. Josh and everybody else would think he was completely out of his mind.

"It's time for you to head off to work," said Alice. "Take as much time as you need to think about it. If you decide you don't want me to move in, I swear to you, I won't get mad or upset. Be honest about what you want."

"I will."

"I love you, Nate."

"I love you, too."

She gave him a gentle kiss and sent him on his way.

JOSH HAD DARK CIRCLES UNDER HIS EYES, LIKE HE'D HAD A TERRIBLE night's sleep. And he'd missed a couple of spots while shaving.

"I guess you heard," he said, giving Nate a pained smile.

"Yep," said Nate. "Dumbass."

"You're supposed to text before you show up at somebody's place! That's the social contract! What if I'd had fumigators there?"

"Fumigators?"

"The people who fumigate."

"I know what fumigators are. But I'm pretty sure that's not why people text before they come over."

"It's just one random example."

"Josh, you're my best friend in the whole wide world, so I'm going to be very direct and say that having sex with another woman is a bigger *faux pas* than not texting."

"We weren't having sex when she got there. We were finished."

"Not really my point."

"Alice made things worse."

"How?"

"Stacey called her up to tell her that I was a cheating piece of shit, and Alice completely took my side. So Stacey was robbed of her chance to vent, and she got madder and madder and came back over to my place."

"With a weapon?"

"No, with her voice. Her angry, angry voice. Do you know how long she screamed at me?"

"Forty-five minutes?"

"More like ten, but still, it was really loud."

"You made your own problem," Nate said.

"I know, I know."

"Are you going to keep seeing Gretchen?"

"I guess we'll keep hooking up, even though we can't stand each other. Her new thing is telling me I'm gay while we're in the midst of heterosexual sex. And she keeps telling me I have a tiny dick, even though I totally don't."

"You may want to spend some time reflecting on the decisions you've made about your love life."

"You're probably right. How are things with Alice?"

"Great," said Nate. He didn't want to mention the idea that they might be moving in together. Josh would aggressively warn him against doing such a thing, and Nate wasn't in the mood to listen to that right now. He hadn't yet decided what to do, and Josh saying "No! No! No! No! No, you fool!" wouldn't be helpful.

It was too soon for him and Alice to make this kind of commitment. Yes, she'd insisted that she'd move out if things didn't work out...but *would* she? This was the kind of decision you made months—years—into a relationship, not two weeks. There was a ton of stuff they didn't know about each other. They might discover they got on each other's nerves constantly.

Some guys would go nuts over the idea of their girlfriend granting them permission to have sex with other women as long as they played it cool. And...yeah, Nate had to admit that there was a "fantasy come true" element to the idea. But it came off like some-thing she'd proposed out of desperation.

Why would she do that? He was nothing special. He was a restaurant server. Surely she didn't think that *Frank, Frank, & Frank* was her key to a life of wealth and luxury. She could attract other guys. Why was she so anxious to keep him that she granted him permission to sleep around?

They had a connection for sure. But it wasn't a deep, spiritual connection where they couldn't imagine spending their lives with anybody else. At least, that isn't how he felt, and Alice hadn't given any indication that she thought he was her destiny. Maybe she hated casual dating so much that she'd do anything to avoid it, and if she found a halfway-decent guy like Nate, she intended to keep him.

The truth was, he didn't want her to move in with him yet.

And though he was very much a "go with the flow" kind of guy, perhaps even too passive for his own good, he needed to be very honest with Alice and tell her that this was too big of a step.

If she needed somewhere to stay *while* she was looking for a new place, that was totally fine. And, of course, he'd help her move all the boxes and furniture. He'd be a top-notch boyfriend in all matters regarding the move. He just wasn't the kind of impulsive guy who would live with his girlfriend when they were still in the early getting-to-know-each-other phase.

She'd understand. And if she didn't...well, that was the kind of red flag it was good to see early.

They were now at the point where it was naturally understood they'd be getting together after he got off work. All he did was text: *Your place?* She texted back a thumbs-up emoji.

He was surprised by how nervous he was when he left the restaurant and got into his car. He shouldn't be. Alice might be disappointed, but she wasn't going to shriek like a banshee and grab a butcher knife out of a drawer. It would be totally fine.

Nate remained nervous for the entire drive.

When he arrived at her house, he grabbed his overnight bag, then walked to her front door and knocked, even though she kept it unlocked when she was home. See? They weren't even at the "just walk right in" phase of their relationship yet. It would be ridiculous for her to get upset with him.

Alice answered the door. She threw her arms around him and gave him a passionate kiss as she not-so-gently led him into the house. She kicked the door shut behind him and tugged up his shirt.

When she pulled her lips away for a moment, Nate said, "I should get a shower."

"You can shower afterward," she told him, removing his shirt and tossing it onto the floor. They didn't make it to the bedroom, or even the couch, instead getting down and dirty right there on the rug in the foyer.

It wasn't a very comfortable place to cuddle afterward—or, truthfully, to have sex—so they moved to the couch for the post-coital rest.

This would not be a good time to tell her about his living-together decision. He should wait until they were dressed.

"Have you thought about it?" Alice asked.

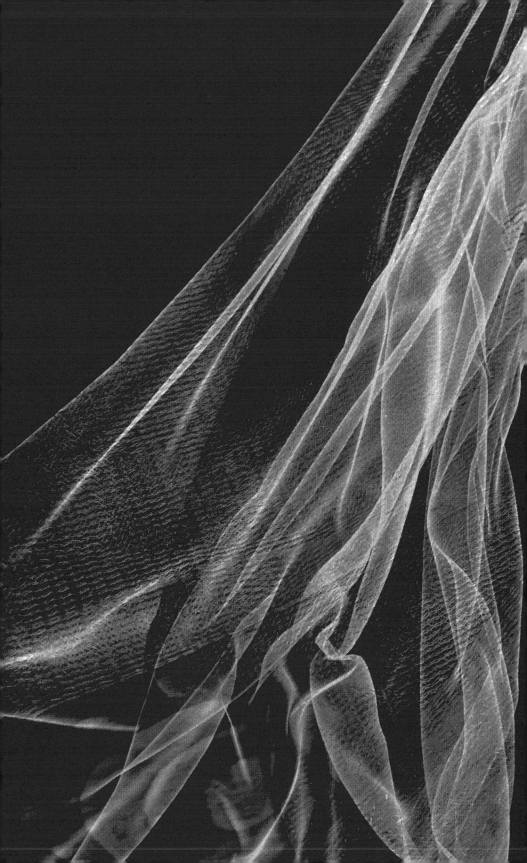

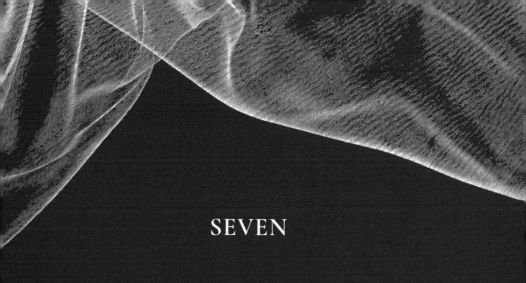

SEVEN

"About what?" Nate asked, which was such a truly idiotic answer that he was ashamed of himself for using that delaying tactic.

"Moving in together."

"Yeah."

"Yeah, you've thought about it?"

"Right. We shouldn't talk about this while we're sitting here naked. I'm still covered in grease from work, so I should get a quick shower. Is that okay?"

"Of course," said Alice.

Nate stood up. He hoped she'd do something playful, like slap him on the ass, to let him know that everything was going to be fine even if he didn't give her the answer she wanted, but she left his ass completely un-slapped as he went into the bathroom.

He took a longer shower than usual, hoping to postpone the conversation.

What if she cried?

What if she just went completely silent?

There was no reason for him to be this worried. Not wanting her to move in with him didn't mean he was a selfish piece of shit.

He was probably stressing out over this for nothing. Most likely, he'd tell Alice his decision, she'd tell him she completely understood, then she'd say it wasn't fair of her to have asked him in the first place, and he'd assure her it was totally fine that she asked, and that he didn't mean he'd *never* want them to live together—it just wasn't a good idea to rush into things. Then they'd make some popcorn and start watching a movie they wouldn't finish.

He got out of the shower, spent longer than necessary drying himself off, got dressed, and then emerged from the bathroom. Alice was *right there*, making him flinch.

"Sorry," she said, taking a step back. "Didn't mean to scare you."

"Well, you didn't scare me, you startled me," said Nate.

"Same thing."

"You're right."

"I don't want to know your answer," said Alice. "This thing with my landlady has put my stomach in knots all day. I hate moving—hate, hate, *hate* it—and I don't want to deal with it right now. I just want to get away from everything. I'd like us to go on vacation together. Not a long one. Three or four days. I'll pay for everything."

"Where to?"

"I have a great deal on a hotel and flights to Las Vegas. Have you ever been?"

"I went with my parents when I was a kid. I sat right outside the casino for hours while my mom played the slot machines."

"That's really sad."

Nate shrugged. "I had a book."

"We don't have to gamble. There's plenty of other stuff to do.

We could eat at some nice restaurants, see a couple of shows, get a room with a hot tub…"

"I'm in. When were you thinking about leaving?"

"Tomorrow morning."

"Oh," said Nate.

"Too soon?"

"I have to work. I have Thursday and Friday off, and I could probably get approved for Saturday and Sunday if they can find somebody to take my shift."

"Can you call in sick?"

"Well, yeah."

"We can stay off social media. I won't ruin your alibi if you don't."

"It's very tempting."

"We can also wait until your days off. But the whole point was to get the hell out of town now before I have a nervous breakdown."

"No, no, I totally get it," said Nate. "Let's do it. I feel a sore throat coming on as we speak."

"Perfect!" said Alice, beaming. "You should go home and pack. Our flight leaves tomorrow morning at 7:20."

"You already bought the tickets?"

"No, I'm on the last step. I was waiting on you before I clicked 'purchase.' But this is going to be so much fun, I promise!"

She gave him a great big kiss, then returned to the living room.

Nate didn't really own anything in the way of fancy attire, but he had four days' worth of stuff that he thought was passable. He hadn't taken an actual vacation in a long time, so he was really looking forward to this. There was a nagging concern that at the end of this trip, he'd look like even *more* of an asshole for saying that Alice couldn't live with him, but she'd specifically said that she didn't want to know his answer yet. If she wanted to take a few days to completely forget about real-world problems, he was all for it.

They took separate Ubers to the airport but met at check-in. The line was mercifully short, as was the security line, at least by the standards of Atlanta International Airport. Alice went ahead of him into the scanner, raising her hands in the appropriate position as the machine did its thing.

"I'm sorry, ma'am," said the TSA agent. "I think it's your necklace."

"Oh."

"Take it off, and we'll scan you again."

Alice pinched the eyeball necklace between her thumb and index finger. "I can't leave it on?"

"We can take you to a private screening, ma'am."

"Let's do that." She glanced over at Nate. "That's okay, right?"

"Sure, no problem at all," Nate said.

Alice left with the agent. Nate went through the scanner without incident, then went to a bench to put his shoes and belt back on.

"Sorry," said Alice, rejoining him a few minutes later. "This thing is a bitch to get back on after I take it off."

"It's okay. We got through the lines so fast that we're just gonna sit at the gate for an hour and a half anyway."

"It's an ugly-ass necklace. I told you the story of it, right?"

"No."

"My mom gave it to me right before she died. She made my dad go out and buy it, and he had terrible taste in jewelry. She'd just told him to get something with an eye on it. She gave it to me and said that it meant she was always watching over me. It's stupid, but I don't like to take it off."

"That's not stupid at all," said Nate.

"But also, it really is a bitch to get back on. The clasp is bent or something. I don't actually believe my mom is watching over me from beyond the grave, or that this necklace symbolizes anything, but I feel sad when I'm not wearing it."

"I completely understand."

"Do you have anything from your father like that?" Alice asked.

Nate shook his head. "He went quickly. I wasn't even home when it happened—I was at school. My mom...actually, this is really fucked up. It's not something to talk about at the start of our vacation."

"Tell me. It's okay."

Nate took a deep breath and exhaled. He hated sharing this story. "When I got home from school, he was already long gone. My mom couldn't handle telling me that Dad was dead, but I obviously knew something was wrong because she couldn't stop crying. so instead, she told me he'd left us."

"Oh my God."

"She kept that up for three days. For three days I thought my dad had just packed up and left us. Had my aunt not intervened, she might never have told me the truth. To this day, she doesn't think she did anything wrong. As you may have guessed, that's part of why we don't have a very good relationship."

"Only part?"

"Yeah, I mean, there's also the whole, 'Why the hell are you wasting time writing plays?' thing. I tried to fly her out to see my one-act, and she said it would depress her. To summarize, my mom sucks. Now, let's talk about what we're going to do in Vegas."

Alice grinned. "Everything we can."

NATE WAS NO FAN OF AIR TRAVEL, AND HE GOT STUCK IN THE MIDDLE seat next to a man with sub-par hygiene (though, to be fair, Alice offered multiple times to swap). She'd suggested they join the Mile-High Club in the bathroom, but there seemed to always be somebody waiting to use it, or else the beverage cart was in the way, and it didn't seem like they could make it happen without everybody in the plane knowing exactly what was going on. Also, despite being young and agile, Nate was worried that thrusting away in those cramped quarters was a good way to get an injury that would cast a pall over the rest of the trip.

Their hotel room was small, but it did indeed have a hot tub.

They had lunch at an amazing buffet, where they both behaved in a responsible manner and stopped eating before they were completely stuffed, at least until they saw the dessert selection. They did some casino-hopping, where Nate won two hundred dollars on a single spin and proceeded to lose it all on subsequent spins. They went to a comedy show that was pretty bad, and then, on Alice's urging, to a strip club where she bought him a lap dance. That was followed by the best steak dinner Nate had eaten in his entire life. Back in the hotel, they spent way too long trying to figure out how to get the bubbles to work in the hot tub, and then made good use of it while polishing off a bottle of red wine. They dried off and got in bed. They were both still quite full, so they didn't bounce as much as they otherwise might, but much more sex was had before they both passed out.

The next day was more of the same, except that Nate did not win two hundred dollars, and he bought a lap dance for Alice. "I'm still not bi," she admitted as they left, "but that was fun." They went to a mystery dinner theater, where Nate was entirely convinced he'd figured out whodunnit, but was completely wrong.

"I don't think their solution works," he said as they walked down the sidewalk.

"What was wrong with it?" Alice asked.

"Do visitor passes actually just have a great big V on them?"

"Some do, I think."

"I've never seen one like that."

"How many visitor passes have you seen?"

"Are you sure they make them like that? Just a V? Nothing else?"

"I think so."

"That doesn't sound right."

"We could look it up."

"No, I want to stay annoyed."

"What do you want to do next, besides staying annoyed?"

"Let's lose some more money in the slot machines."

After losing another twenty dollars each in the slots, Alice suggested they get some drinks. That sounded like a perfectly fine idea. Nate didn't drink much for a single guy in his twenties, but that didn't mean he wasn't ready to indulge here in Vegas.

They stopped at a small bar that specialized in margaritas. A guy played acoustic guitar up front, singing unrecognizable versions of contemporary hits. Nate and Alice each had a drink, and then a second, and then—because they didn't taste like there was that much alcohol in them—a third.

"I think I'm drunk," said Alice.

"You may be right."

"I'm scared to get off the stool."

"I'll help you."

"No, you're drunk too."

"Not as drunk as you are."

"We're both too drunk to get off these high stools. We'll fall and break dozens of bones and ruin our whole trip. We're trapped here forever."

"That bites," said Nate.

"Yeah. At least we can have more drinks while we're trapped here."

"Mmmmm."

"Wanna know a secret?" Alice asked.

"Sure."

"I love you."

"I love you, too."

"Do you?"

"Yeah."

"Good. Unrequited love sucks. And I must not be as drunk as I thought if I can say 'unrequited.' Unrequited. Unrequited. Unrequited."

"The big black blug bleegs..." said Nate.

"What are you saying?"

"It's a tongue-twister. The big black bug bleegs blag..."

"I have no idea what you're trying to say," said Alice.

"The. Big. Black. Bug. Bleeds. Black. Blug—I mean, blood."

"I'm not even going to try to say that."

"Toy boat," said Nate. "Toy boat. Toy boyt. Shit."

"She sells seashells by the seashore. Ha!"

"Say 'toy boat' ten times fast."

"No."

"Ten times slow."

"No."

"You're no fun."

"I'm super fun," said Alice.

"That's true."

"How are you feeling?"

"Happy."

"Me too."

"I don't think I'm that drunk," said Nate. "I'm not saying I'm sober. That would be a lie. But I'm more buzzed than drunk. Or, what's the level between buzzed and drunk?"

"Tipsy?"

"That's it. I'm tipsy. Or maybe I'm drunk. No, I think I'm just tipsy."

"Are you feeling crazy?"

"I'm always feeling crazy."

"Are you feeling...impulsive?"

"Maybe."

"Let's be impulsive, Nate."

"Like, tattoos?"

"Or rings."

"Rings?"

"Rings."

"Onion rings?"

"I think we should be wild," said Alice. "We should live without a safety net. Let's do what feels right and not worry about what anybody else thinks. Let's do something just for us."

"What did you have in mind?"

Alice leaned over and gave him a big kiss on the lips. "Let's get fucking married."

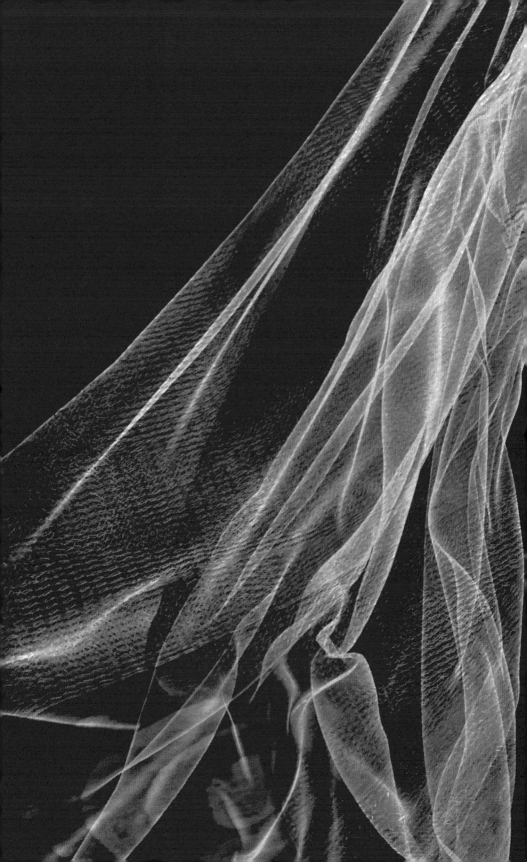

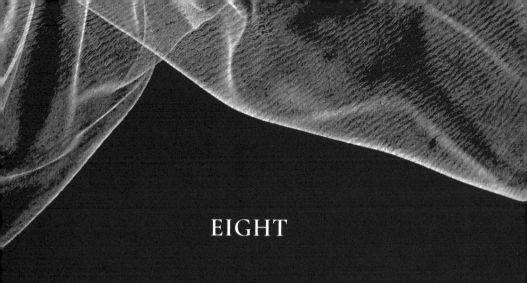

EIGHT

N ate laughed. "Yeah, right."

"We're in love, aren't we?"

"Yeah."

"We get along great. We get along *perfectly*, if you ask me. I've never felt this way about anybody before. I look at you and I know I want us to spend the rest of our lives together. And I know you feel the same way about me."

Nate didn't answer. He suddenly wished he hadn't had that third margarita.

"Life is short," Alice said. "And I'll be the best wife you can imagine. Let's do this."

"Are you messing with me?"

"I mean every word I'm saying right now. I want to get married. I want to find one of those twenty-four-hour wedding chapels and marry you."

Nate laughed again. "We're not getting married tonight."

Alice's expression turned deadly serious. "Don't you laugh at

"I'm just—"

"I mean it. Don't laugh at me. Don't act like this is a big fucking joke."

Nate leaned back, flustered. He almost fell off the stool but steadied himself before that could happen. "Okay, I'm confused here. You suddenly blurt out that you want us to get married, and I'm supposed to take you seriously?"

"Why are you so scared?"

"I'm not scared. We've only been together for three weeks, Alice."

"Three amazing weeks."

"But still, three weeks. I'm not even ready for us to move in together, so I'm definitely not ready for us to get married. That's insane."

"It's where we're headed," said Alice. "So why wait? Don't you want to be able to look back when we're in our nineties and laugh about how we did something crazy and wonderful?"

"I think you're too drunk to be making these decisions."

Alice took both of his hands in hers. "I'm not. I swear. This isn't the alcohol talking. What we have together is special, Nate. It's unique. It's almost otherworldly. You can't tell me you don't see it."

"Even if I do, that doesn't mean we have to get married. We can't just run down the street and find a chapel. What about our families?"

"You hate your mother."

"I don't *hate* my mother. And maybe telling her that I'm getting married, in a normal amount of time, is something that could bring us closer together. What about your dad? What about Josh?"

"Do you really think Josh would cry if he didn't get to come to our wedding?"

"He wouldn't cry. He'd be a little pissed."

"He can do a bachelor party afterward. Hell, we can do a

friends-and-family wedding later and invite anybody you want. Let's do this just for us. Just us. We deserve it."

"Maybe, but—"

"I have money saved. A lot of it. We could take a really long honeymoon. You could take a leave of absence from your job and just write. Wouldn't that be incredible?"

"I'm sorry," said Nate. "I care about you, and it's easy to envision a long future for us, but I'm not marrying you tonight. End of discussion."

She looked at him like he'd slapped her across the face. "End of discussion, huh? We're not even going to talk about this like adults?"

"Right! There's nothing to talk about! It's like if I suggested that we rob this place. We wouldn't need to sit here and do a full analysis to figure out that it was completely nuts."

Alice wiped a tear from her eye. "I didn't realize you were so selfish."

"Selfish? How am I selfish? Why do I even need to explain this? Why isn't it obvious to you what the problem is with this whole idea? When you sober up, you'll realize how ridiculous you're being. If you're feeling wild and reckless and drunk and you want to propose—fine! On some level I admire that. But don't get pissed at me if I don't go along with it."

Alice just stared at him. Tears trickled down her cheeks, her mouth quivered, and she looked as if she was building up to let out a huge shriek of anguish.

But she didn't. She sat there and wept.

Nate didn't turn to look, but he could almost feel the other people in the bar staring at them. His face burned.

He felt awful. He shouldn't—if anything, she was the one who should feel bad for putting him in this position. If she genuinely thought he was being a selfish prick, then there was something deeply wrong with her. They'd crossed the line from "endearingly quirky" to "run, you poor son of a bitch, run!"

"Let's just go back to the room," he said.

"You think I'm going to fuck you after this?"

"No. That's not at all what I meant, and you know it. I think...I think we just need to sleep this off, and see how we feel after a good night's rest and some coffee."

"You can go back to the room," said Alice. "I need some time to get over being kicked in the face."

"I didn't break up with you! All I did was..." Nate trailed off. "I don't need to keep justifying my decision. If you think I'm the bad guy, that's fine. Clearly I'm not going to change your mind right now."

Alice got off the stool. "I'll see you later, maybe."

"Where are you going?"

"To walk around."

"You shouldn't walk around Vegas by yourself at night."

"You can't tell me what to do. You're not my husband."

"I'm still your boyfriend."

"Well, that doesn't do me a goddamn bit of good, does it? You've ruined everything. Go to hell."

All right. In the event that they somehow stayed together after this—which was *extremely* unlikely—Nate knew that margaritas were not Alice's friend.

She stormed off. Nate hurriedly followed her.

"Don't go," he said, gently grabbing her arm.

"Let go of me, or I'll fucking scream," she told him.

Nate immediately let her go. As she left, he remembered that he still had to pay for the drinks, so he sheepishly returned to the bar and settled his tab. Everybody was indeed staring at him.

Well...he supposed it was good to know this about her now, before things got even more serious.

He left the bar, hoping she'd be waiting outside. She wasn't.
Wow.

Holy freaking crap. He was dating a psychopath.

Was it even safe to sleep in the hotel tonight? Would he wake up with a knife to his throat and a wedding band around his finger? *"Oh, you will marry me, my sweet lover, or your sweet crimson blood will spill all over these white sheets."*

Okay, "psychopath" was going too far. For one thing, Alice was drunk. When she sobered up, she'd apologize for her behavior, if she even remembered it.

Then he'd give her a hug, apologize for his own behavior—even though he believed he'd been acting like a rational human being—try to enjoy the rest of the trip, and then break up with her when they returned to Atlanta. Nate really didn't see how they could smooth this over to the point where he felt it was wise continuing to be Alice's boyfriend.

He felt terrible, because she clearly had a major tragedy in her past; one that might be messing with her ability to have a normal relationship. The three Franks in *Frank, Frank & Frank* all had backstories that impacted their current behavior. But he hadn't signed on for this level of drama. As much as he liked Alice, he was starting to think that maybe he didn't want a steady girlfriend at this time in his life.

That was all for later. Right now, it worried him to have an intoxicated, angry Alice wandering around Las Vegas at night. If she stuck to the strip, she'd probably be fine, but he didn't know where she might go. Hopefully she'd just head back to the hotel and go to sleep.

If you need me to come get you anywhere, just let me know, he texted.

He could see that she immediately read the message. But she didn't respond.

There wasn't much he could do now. He didn't want to sit in an empty hotel room, so he decided to wander Las Vegas by himself. No more drinking, though.

He got a pretty good chili dog, then did some joyless gambling at a slot machine. After losing twenty bucks with remarkable haste, he walked over to a craps table. He watched for a few minutes but couldn't understand the rules, so he went over to the bar and ordered a Diet Coke.

"Oooh, big drinker," said the woman on the stool next to him. She wore a sequined black dress and gave off a very strong "high-priced escort" vibe.

"Totally," said Nate. "I'm out of control."

"You look troubled."

"A little, yeah."

"Is it something I can help you with?"

"Nah."

"You sure? I'm a great listener. And a great distractor."

"Even if I was interested, I can't afford you." Had he really just said that? What if she wasn't an escort?

Instead of slapping the shit out of him, she smiled. "You might be surprised."

"I'm not looking for that kind of company right now."

"Then how about you buy me a drink?"

"I really shouldn't."

"Aw, c'mon, don't be mean."

Nate suddenly had this feeling that he was being watched. He spun around, and there was Alice, watching him talk to a hooker.

No, wait. It wasn't Alice. It barely even looked like her.

He wasn't doing anything wrong, but still, he needed to remove himself from this situation before Alice *did* see him.

"I've gotta go," he told her.

"Here's my card if you change your mind," she said, handing him a card that said: *Eliza. Distraction expert.*

"You have a business card?"

"Sure, why not? If you get lonely, just scan the QR code."

He gave the card back to her. "I'm not interested, but I admire your professionalism." He gulped down his Diet Coke and left.

Then he got that unpleasant fizzy feeling in his nose. He shouldn't have drunk the Coke so quickly.

He got lost on his way out of the casino, which, of course, was by design. He stopped to lose ten bucks in a slot machine, then finally emerged onto the street. It was probably time to just head back to their room. He walked a few blocks in the wrong direction, then retraced his steps and returned to the hotel. He resisted the urge to throw any more money in a slot machine, ignoring the flashing lights and cheers as some lucky motherfucker won a jackpot.

When he entered the room, Alice was sitting on the bed.

Her face was stained with tears, but she wasn't crying at the moment.

"I'm sorry," she said.

"It's okay."

Alice shook her head. "It's not."

"We had too much to drink."

"The margaritas weren't that strong."

"Still, it's okay."

Alice picked up her cell phone and held it up. Nate squinted, then walked over to the bed to see what she was showing him. An X-Ray.

"What's that?" he asked.

"It's me."

Nate peered closer. It did indeed say "Alice Vinestalk" in the upper corner.

"Okay," he said, feeling a bit sick to his stomach. "What exactly am I looking at here?"

"My brain. Isn't it cute?"

"Alice—"

"I know, I know, I shouldn't be joking around. I'll just come right out and say it. I'm dying."

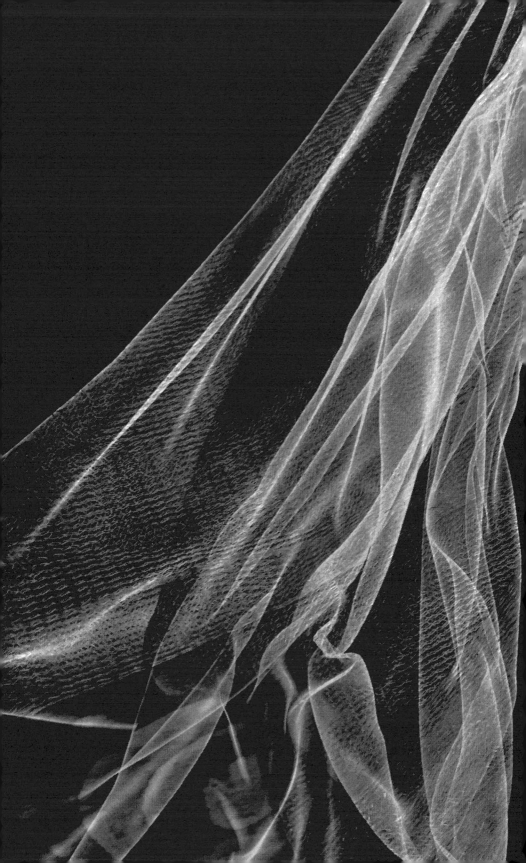

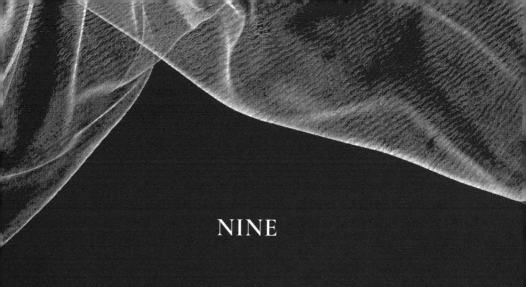

NINE

Nate just stood there for a moment. He tried to speak but his mouth had gone completely dry.

"I beat cancer before," said Alice. "I made it my bitch. But it was a long process, hell on earth, and my husband really wasn't up for the task. He stayed by my side the whole time, but he didn't want to be there, and when I got the all-clear, we knew we were over. We'd just barely made it through losing our daughter. It was an accident. It wasn't either of our faults. Just one of those horrible things that happens sometimes. We'd gotten married because he knocked me up, and we thought our love of Olympia would keep us together, but…"

Alice closed her eyes and took a long, deep breath to compose herself.

"We never had the chance to enjoy each other," she continued. "We went from panicking over the unplanned pregnancy, to the exhaustion of having a newborn, to losing her. A couple of very bad years after that. Then I got sick. Our marriage might not have lasted even if Olympia had lived, and I was completely healthy, but under those conditions we didn't really stand a chance. I haven't spoken to him since the divorce."

Nate wanted to say, "I'm sorry," but that seemed incredibly lame and inadequate. He also wanted to put a hand on her shoulder, or do something to comfort her, but he couldn't seem to make himself move. Instead, he continued standing there, letting her speak.

"Anyway, I'm sick again. Late stage. Breast cancer that's metastasized into my brain. With a lot of chemotherapy and radiation, I have a teeny tiny little chance of beating it. The odds are so far against me that I don't want to go through it again. I just don't. I want to enjoy the time I have left and go out with some dignity."

"How long do you have?" asked Nate.

Alice shrugged. "A year at the absolute most, if I'm really lucky."

"Jesus." He sat down next to her on the bed. "I can't even imagine what this is like for you."

She gave him a sad smile. "It's not great."

"I'm glad you told me."

"I should've told you sooner. It's just really hard, you know? I have a lot of living to cram into a ridiculously short amount of time, and when I met you I felt like we had this amazing connection. I wanted to experience everything I could with you before my time ran out. I wanted us to get married, and go on adventures, and wring everything we possibly could out of this life before the end. I should have told you. I tried. I tried so many times. I just couldn't force myself. And then I fucked everything up."

"No, you didn't."

"Of course I did. I asked you to marry me, and then I had a meltdown when you didn't. It wasn't fair to put you in that position. It was manipulative. It was shitty. What if you'd said yes? What if we'd gone through with it? *Then* I was going to tell you that this was a short-term marriage? I'm a fucking wreck, Nate, and I let the charade that everything was fine get away from me. I'm so sorry. I don't expect you to forgive me."

"It's okay," said Nate.

"It's not okay. Not even a little."

"You've gone through hell. I don't know how I'd behave in your position."

"Better than me, probably."

"I don't know. I mean, I haven't had the best life ever. There's definitely some darkness in there. But if you asked me what a bad day looked like for me now, it would be a customer yelling at me because his nachos didn't have enough queso, or a sucky blind date. Nothing like what you're going through."

"I was still horrible to you," said Alice. "I can explain it, but I can't excuse it. All I can say is that I feel this connection to you. I don't know if you feel it. It's okay if you don't. When we went out for burgers, I was at peace, and I hadn't felt that way in a really long time. I'm not religious, not really, but I could almost believe you were sent to me by a higher power. I know that sounds corny. Don't go getting a big head, I don't mean that you're this heaven-sent angel, but we got along so well, and I fell in love with you, and I knew you were the one who could make me happy."

Nate took her hand. "That's all I wanted to do."

"But the lies stop now, I promise," said Alice. "I guess I wasn't lying. I was withholding information. Is there anything else you want to know?"

Nate almost didn't ask. But if he asked now, while things were already emotionally charged, he wouldn't have to ever bring it up again. "What happened to Olympia?"

Alice bit her lip. It took her a moment to speak. "She found a pretty rock and put it in her pocket. We forgot to take it away from her when we got home." She looked down at her lap and went silent.

"It's all right," said Nate. "You don't have to keep going."

Alice shook her head. "You deserve to know. We'd childproofed the entire downstairs, but we forgot about that one goddamn rock. We couldn't get it out of her throat. It just would not come out. She bit down on my finger so hard I needed stitches, and in those last moments, where her face was completely blue, my husband was so frantic with the Heimlich Maneuver that he...that he broke three of her ribs."

Nate wanted to say something reassuring, but he couldn't speak.

Alice wiped a tear from her eye. "So, yeah, it was a less than ideal time in my life."

"Oh, God, Alice, I'm so sorry."

"You weren't there. You didn't give her the rock."

"You know what I mean."

"I know." She pulled some tissue out of her pocket and wiped her nose. "I think that about covers it. To recap: Shitty parent. Shitty girlfriend. Dead soon."

"You're none of those things," said Nate.

"I'm the last one, at least. Unless you're a cancer-removing sorcerer."

"Fine. But you're not shitty."

"I think that's the most romantic thing anybody's ever said to me."

Nate smiled. "You're welcome."

"Anyway, I'm sorry I ruined our trip. Losing my house, on top of everything else, put me in this weird, unhealthy mental space, and I thought taking this trip would help, and it did, until I went insane and thought you'd actually marry me. So, I'm sorry. And also, I will never drink another margarita."

"That's probably for the best," Nate admitted.

"So where do we go from here?"

"I honestly have no idea."

"Are we over?" Alice asked.

"Absolutely not." It all made sense now. She wasn't insane. She was going through a nightmare that Nate couldn't even imagine. When you had so little time left, you didn't want to waste any of it. You'd want to accelerate the timeframe of…well, stuff like getting married.

If he found out he was dying of cancer, he wouldn't behave in the most rational manner, either.

"You can leave if you want," said Alice. "I won't hold it against you."

"Not a chance. You can't get rid of me that easily. I don't know about you, but I'm tired as hell."

"I'm exhausted."

"So let's get some sleep, and then we'll do a reset in the morning."

"I'd really, really like that."

They took separate showers, then climbed into bed together. They didn't make love, but Alice fell asleep in his arms.

Nate couldn't fall asleep.

He kept thinking about the whole evening, especially the part about doing something crazy and wonderful.

Marrying her would be nuts.

And it would end in heartbreak. Soon.

But they could share a lot of happiness before the end. The really long honeymoon had definite appeal, as did the opportunity to just write for a while. Hell, maybe he could write a play about their lives.

He couldn't believe he was actually considering this.

Nate wasn't spontaneous. He didn't do crazy shit. He was meticulous about safe sex, and he filed his taxes on time.

They could make some incredible memories in her remaining time.

Not that they needed to get married to make memories.

But, God, it would make her so happy.

If she was lying about all of this, he could get an annulment. And if she wasn't...it felt evil to think of it in these terms, but it wasn't a long commitment.

That was horrible.

Yet accurate.

He refused to think of it in those terms. *"If it doesn't work out, she'll be dead soon anyway."* That was fucked up. He needed to think of it in terms of a wild and reckless adventure.

So what if Josh would think he lost his mind? Josh didn't exactly have his own life in order.

Nate had nobody to answer to.

And was this actually starting to feel...right?

Maybe it was the high emotions of the day. Maybe it was the alcohol. But he was starting to think he might actually do this.

He finally fell asleep with Alice still in his arms.

NATE WOKE UP THE NEXT MORNING, BLISSFULLY HANGOVER-FREE. Alice sat at the desk, wearing a robe, drinking a cup of coffee.

"Good morning, sleepyhead," she said.

"Good morning." Nate sat up. "How long have you been up?"

"Not too long. About half an hour. Just sitting here, thinking."

"About what?"

"I'm done with Vegas. What if we rented a car and drove to the Grand Canyon? I've never been there. Have you?"

"Nope."

"The West Rim is only two and a half hours away. I don't know the difference between the rims, but ultimately it's just a big hole. One rim is as good as another."

"That sounds kind of filthy," said Nate.

"Completely not my intention."

"I could go for a trip to the Grand Canyon. It'll keep me from losing more money in the slots."

"Then let's do it. I'll rent a car online. Do you want me to make you a cup of coffee?"

"Yeah, thanks."

Nate went to the bathroom, brushed his teeth, and got dressed. He sat on the edge of the bed and sipped his coffee while Alice rented a car. With caffeine entering his system instead of alcohol, his mind was clear.

He still wanted to do this.

He finished the entire cup just to be sure.

Yes, he still wanted to do this.

Madness.

But wonderful madness.

How should he do this? Should he drop to one knee and propose? Should he try to come up with something clever? Should he say, "Yo, babe, I changed my mind"?

He stood up, walked over to where she sat, and got down on one knee.

Alice stared at him. Her mouth fell open.

"I'd think you were tying your shoes, but you aren't wearing any."

"Alice," Nate said, his throat suddenly very dry, "we haven't known each other very long, but I feel like I've known you forever. I don't have a ring. Now that I'm down here, I wish I'd made one out of paper or something. But missing ring notwithstanding, I wanted to ask if you'd do me the honor of being my wife?"

"Are you fucking with me?" Alice asked.

"No. I am not fucking with you."

She put her hand over her mouth and let out a half-laugh, half-gasp. "Are you serious? Are you really serious?"

"Totally serious."

"What made you—no, don't answer that. Yes, Nate! Yes, I'll marry you!"

She burst into tears.

"Those are happy tears, right?" Nate asked.

Alice nodded so vigorously that Nate worried she might hurt her neck. "Yes! They're happy tears! Oh, God, they're the happiest tears you can imagine!"

Nate stood up, and Alice stood up, and they embraced. She hugged him tight.

"Whoa," he said. "Don't break my—"

He stopped himself before he could finish his joke about her breaking his ribs. Shit! Had he completely destroyed the celebratory mood?

Alice didn't seem to have noticed. She kept him in the bear hug for quite a while, then released him and covered his face with kisses.

"Do you mean today?" she asked, looking positively elated.

"Yes."

She burst into tears again.

"Let's go," she said, taking his hand. "I want to get hitched before you change your mind, soon-to-be husband of mine."

THEY COULD HAVE BEEN MARRIED BY AN ELVIS IMPERSONATOR, BUT neither of them wanted to go that route, so they went with a regular justice of the peace. Alice had already filled out the forms online, and Nate was surprised at the ease and speed of the process. They didn't have a witness, but the chapel provided an old lady to watch them exchange vows, nodding her approval.

During the very brief ceremony, Nate wondered what the hell he was doing, but he went through with it. And when he kissed his bride, he felt like, yeah, this was the right thing to do.

As they walked out of the chapel, husband and wife, Alice let out a great big sigh of relief.

"What was that for?" asked Nate, amused.

"I thought you might run for your life before they finished the job."

"Nah." Nate fiddled with the ring. The chapel had very inexpensive rings available, so they bought a couple of those, with the intention of upgrading when they got back home. ("Or not," said Alice. "I don't really care about the ring. I only care about us.")

"Let's skip the Grand Canyon," said Alice. "Plenty of adventures await us in our very own hotel room."

That idea sounded perfectly good to Nate.

"And can we save the calls to family until we get back home?" she asked. "Let's enjoy this together. Just you and me."

"Absolutely." To be honest, now that the deed was done, Nate was kind of dreading telling Josh. His friend would probably try to check him into a psychiatric facility.

Minutes after they returned to their room, he lay on top of her, nibbling his wife's—holy shit!—ear as he gently thrust into her. She made soft sounds of pleasure for a couple of minutes, and then began to tremble.

Was she crying?

"Are you okay?" he asked.

Alice nodded. "Just emotional. Keep going."

They got a tremendous amount of use out of that bed, with a break to order room service for lunch. Then they got even more use out of the bed.

Afterward, Nate was completely spent. He hoped Alice was satisfied, because he had nothing left. She left his exhausted body on the bed while she took a quick shower. When she emerged, she was fully clothed.

"Going somewhere?" Nate asked.

"No. Just wanted to get dressed." She stared at him for a moment. "Maybe you should get dressed, too."

"Why?"

"I just think maybe you should get dressed."

Did she have a surprise planned for him? Nate got out of bed. "Do I need to take a shower?"

"No."

Nate opened the drawer and took out some clean clothes. She was still looking at him. Her expression was indecipherable.

"What?" he asked.

"Huh?"

"You're acting weird."

She gave him a smile that felt completely forced. "I always act weird."

"Weirder than normal."

"Please just get dressed."

Nate put on his boxer shorts and socks. The mood had changed in a big way. What the hell was wrong? Had it suddenly sunk in to Alice that she was married to a dumbass like him? Was she having second thoughts?

She kept staring at him as he put on his jeans and T-shirt.

"Okay," he said, "I'm dressed."

"I love you, Nate."

"I love you too."

"I mean it. My feelings for you are real."

"Is there a reason I should think they aren't?"

"Yes."

What the fuck?

"I have no idea what's happening right now," he admitted.

"I know." Alice closed her eyes and breathed in through her nose, as if gathering courage. "I have a lot of explaining to do."

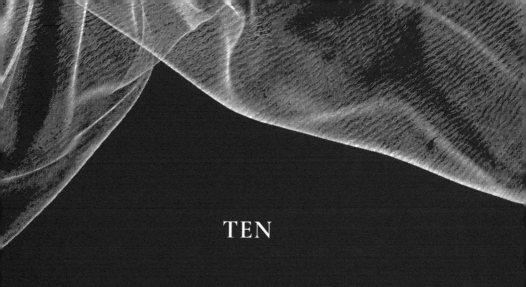

TEN

Alice's ears were ringing from the sound of the gunshot. Cindy's blood had gotten on her face and shirt.

"She didn't do anything!" Alice wailed.

The man in the black facemask pointed the gun at her. "That was to prove we're serious. Do you agree that we're serious?"

Alice nodded.

"Touch her," the man said.

"What?"

"Touch the body."

"*What?*"

"Touch the goddamn body, or I'll shoot you in the fucking head."

Alice knelt down beside her sister's dead body. Blood was pooling on the cement floor of the garage. She gently pressed her index finger to Cindy's shoulder.

"Not like that." The man crouched down, grabbed Alice's hand, and shoved it against the bullet hole in Cindy's forehead. "Like that! Dig your finger in there!"

"Please—!"

"I need you to recognize that this is really happening. After we let you go, I don't want you to think that maybe it was a fake-out. Once you're safe, you might decide that Cindy was in on it, and she used special effects or something and only *pretended* to get shot. So jam your finger in there deep, and swirl it all around."

"Please don't make me do this."

"The other option is that I bring Olympia and Peter out here and execute them just like I did their aunt. Of course, if I do that, this has all been one great big waste of time. But if you're not going to cooperate, it's a waste of time anyway."

Alice did as she was told, somehow managing not to vomit.

"Here," said the man, flinging a white rag at her. "Wipe yourself off."

She cleaned up her finger as well as she could. The man didn't offer to take the rag back from her, so she dropped it on the floor.

"You understand that the stakes are real, right? This is not a bluff. We *will* murder your children."

"I understand."

The man smiled. Through the mouth hole in the facemask, she could see his yellow teeth. "Good. Follow me."

"I NEED YOU TO PROMISE ME SOMETHING," ALICE TOLD NATE. "I'M going to tell you everything, and a lot of it will make you really upset and angry. You can ask questions, and I'll answer as many of them as I can, but you have to promise to hear me out until the end. You can't just storm out of here. Okay?"

"Okay," said Nate, who was feeling sick to his stomach. He sat down on the bed.

"Promise me."

"I promise I'll hear you out until the end."

"And be patient with me. I've been working out how I was going to tell you this, but now it's all jumbled and confused in my brain."

"I'll listen patiently."

Alice ran her fingers over the eyeball necklace. "This isn't just a necklace. It's a camera."

"Please tell me we're not on a reality show."

"No, no, no, nothing like that. It's surveillance."

"People were watching us fuck?"

"Yes, but—"

"Are you serious? We're having sex while people watch?"

"It's not about that," said Alice. "I don't like it either, but it was a sacrifice I had to make. I just try not to think about it."

"I can't believe this," said Nate. "So we've been making porn all this time? Are people paying to watch?"

"Nate, stop. Calm down. The sex part is not what this is about. I have permission to tell you everything, but I don't *have* to tell you everything, so I need you to relax."

"All right. I'll relax."

"Here," said the man in the facemask, handing her a silver necklace.

"What's this?"

"Put it on."

The necklace was ugly as hell. It had an eyeball for the pendant. It wasn't like anything she'd ever wear, not that she cared about jewelry at the moment.

She tried to put on the necklace, but her hands were trembling and she couldn't fasten the clasp. The man helped her.

"Never take it off," the man said. "I mean, never."

"I won't."

"It has a camera and a microphone in it. We'll be watching and listening all the time. We'll be watching and listening other ways, too, so don't try to be clever. Assume that we can see and hear everything you're doing. If we get suspicious, we won't give you the benefit of the doubt, so if you don't want two dead kids, follow the rules. Do you understand?"

"Yes."

"Good." He tapped the eyeball with his index finger. "I think it suits you. Don't worry about getting it wet—it'll be fine. And the guys who will be monitoring you are total professionals. You don't have to worry about them getting off while you're fucking or taking a shit. Honestly, the best thing you can do is try to put it completely out of your mind."

"Yeah, right."

"I think after the first couple of days you'll get used to it. But again, let me be as clear as humanly possible about this: Do not signal to anybody. Don't try to be sneaky. However you think you're going to discreetly send a message, know that we've thought of it, and the consequences will be severe. Play by the rules. Do you one hundred percent understand?"

"Yes."

The man smiled. "Perfect. Now let's delete some pictures from your social media accounts."

"I LIED TO YOU," SAID ALICE. "MY NAME *IS* ALICE VINESTALK, AND I am divorced. We got divorced because he had an affair with his boss, which the company found out about when she gave him an annual performance review that was completely out of line with his production numbers. I'm not dying of cancer. I'm perfectly healthy."

"Are you..." Nate stopped before he could ask if she was fucking kidding. He'd promised to hear her out.

Alice succumbed to tears.

What was he supposed to do? Console her? Give her a hug? He had absolutely no idea how to behave in a situation where she was explaining how she'd been lying her ass off all this time.

He just sat there helplessly until Alice had regained her composure enough to resume speaking. "I did not lose my daughter."

A flash of anger rushed through Nate. That heartbreaking story was bullshit?

"Don't get mad," she said.

He didn't care if she could see the fury on his face. "What the fuck kind of psychopath are you?" he asked. "You tricked me into marrying you?"

"Yes," Alice admitted. "I did. But I'm not a psychopath."

"I trusted you!"

"I know all of this. Nothing you're saying is a surprise to me. I manipulated you, and tricked you, and betrayed your trust. And if you let me get to the end of my story, like you promised you would, you'll understand everything. Otherwise, I'll just have to leave."

"Fine," he said. "Please, do continue explaining to me how you're a deceptive bitch."

"Call me a bitch again and I'm out of here."

"Whatever."

"I have two children. Olympia is six. Peter is eight. They mean everything to me. I would rather die than let something happen to them. There is nothing—and I mean *nothing*—I won't do to protect my children. I'm sorry I lied to you and conned you into marrying me, but I'd do it all over again, and much worse. I'm a liar, but believe me when I say, there is no limit to how far I'll go to keep them safe."

"All right," said Nate. "I believe you."

Alice looked like she was going to start crying again, but kept herself under control. "They've been kidnapped."

"Seriously?"

"I'm dead serious. And if I hadn't gotten you to marry me, they would've been killed."

"*What?*"

"Okay, I think that'll do it," said the man in the facemask, hovering over Alice's shoulder as she sat at the computer. There'd been a terrifying moment where she couldn't remember her password (she'd only ever checked Facebook from her own phone and laptop), and the man thought she was lying to him, but she'd figured it out.

"I'm on your side," the man had explained as she deleted pictures of Olympia and Peter. "It'll be harder to convince a guy to marry you if you've got bratty kids, or if he thinks your ex will always be in the picture because of some shared custody bullshit. You need to maximize your chances of success."

"Thank you."

"Don't thank me. Some parts of this job are fun. I like breaking fingers. When you twist some asshole's arm behind his back, waiting for the *snap*, it's almost orgasmic. But shooting a couple of little kids in the back of the head is my idea of a terrible day at work. Oh, I'll do it. I've killed a kid before, even younger than Olympia. She was right there in her mother's arms. Credit where it's due—her mom screamed her goddamn head off, but she didn't drop her. That day *sucked.* So if you could not mess this up, I'd appreciate it."

"I won't mess it up."

"LET ME GET THIS STRAIGHT," SAID NATE. "YOU'RE TELLING ME THAT if we didn't get married, somebody would murder your kids?"

Alice nodded. "That's exactly it."

"That's insane!"

"I'm very much aware of that."

"Why didn't you call the cops? Or the FBI?"

"Because that was against the rules. Bring in the cops or a private investigator or anybody like that, and Olympia and Peter were dead. If I told you what was going on, or even hinted at it, they'd be killed. If I told you that we could get the marriage annulled, they'd be killed. If I did anything that wasn't in the spirit of the game, they'd be killed."

"WHAT DOES THAT MEAN?" ALICE ASKED.

"It means, don't cheat," said the man. "Don't offer him a million bucks to marry you. Don't threaten to kill his dog if he doesn't put a ring on that finger. There's plenty of wiggle room, but you have to make him do it willingly. By all means, use your bag of tricks…" The facemask didn't hide the lascivious look he gave her. "…but just make sure you're sticking to the spirit of the game. There will be exactly one warning, and if I have to warn you, the punishment will be that you choose which of your kids I kill. That still leaves you with one kid, which is more than some people have, but I'm guessing you want to avoid that. So err on the side of caution."

"I will."

"If you want, you can choose the kid now and save us some time later."

"Go to hell."

The man immediately pressed the barrel of his revolver against Alice's forehead.

"I'm sorry, I think you misunderstood the power dynamic here. I can give you shit. You cannot give me shit in return. Watch your goddamn mouth, or I'll blow your brains out."

"You're not allowed to kill me."

"You don't think so?"

"No."

The man chuckled. "Willing to bet your life on that? Tell me to go to hell again. Go ahead and tell me. Do it. C'mon. It'll be fun."

Alice said nothing.

"Or...you could apologize for being disrespectful."

"I'm sorry."

"Say it without sounding like you want to rip my throat out."

"I'm sorry for what I said to you."

"Now you sound like you're being sarcastic, but that's fine." The man lowered the gun. "Good call, by the way. I'm not allowed to kill you. But it would make your task a lot harder if I broke both of your legs, don't you think?"

"What's the matter with you?" asked Cindy, as soon as she started the car.

"What do you mean?"

"Don't play dumb. You know exactly what I mean."

Alice shrugged. "What's the big deal?"

"The big deal is that it pissed off Renee."

"And? Renee has hated us since we were kids. She didn't invite us to this party because she wanted us there. She invited us so she could rub her newfound wealth in our faces. And, job well done. Her house is gorgeous. She's rich as hell. She doesn't have to work another day in her life. She wins."

"Right! Because she's married to a criminal."

"We don't know that he's a criminal."

"Oh, no, I'm sure he's a legitimate businessman," said Cindy. "Do you honestly think there aren't bodies at the bottom of lakes because of him?"

"You can't really believe that."

"Did you spend *any* time talking to him?"

"Actually, I didn't."

"Well, I did. And he scared the shit out of me. And Renee scares the shit out of me now that she's married to him."

"Then why did we even go to this party?"

"Because I wanted to see how she lives now and get some free rich-people's food. But I didn't think you'd piss her off like that."

"It was funny. Other people did worse stuff."

"Yes, but the other people aren't her frenemy. Did you see the way she looked at you?"

"I guess I missed it."

"Well, I did see it, and you should call her tomorrow and apologize."

"Screw that."

"I'm serious, Alice. She's dangerous."

"My God. Are you hearing yourself? You sound like a raging lunatic."

"And I'm saying that Renee is both a raging lunatic and married to a raging lunatic with resources. She hates you, Alice. She's hated you since you were five."

"Has it really been that long?"

"Yes!"

"I don't even remember what I did."

"You beat her at hopscotch," said Cindy. "And then you beat her at lots of other things while you were growing up."

"It's not like I was a little bitch about it."

"And then you stole her first boyfriend."

"No," said Alice. "No, I did not. He broke up with her, and then he started flirting with me. There was no spillover."

"That's not the way she saw it."

"Well, she's a paranoid asshole."

"Yes! Exactly! What I'm saying is that she's hated your guts for twenty years, and now she's married to a guy who has absolutely made people disappear, and you humiliated her in front of all of her friends."

"I didn't *humiliate* her."

"In her mind, you did. And that's all that matters."

"I'm not the one who started it! Other people were way worse."

"You've already said that. It doesn't make any difference. She hates *you*, and she looked at *you* like she wanted to murder you, and I guarantee you that she is seething about it right now. You need to make this right. You need to call her and apologize."

"I'll text her."

"No! Call her. Let her know you're sincere."

"I'm not sincere."

"Make her believe that you are."

"Fine," said Alice. "I'll call her up first thing tomorrow and apologize."

The apology was not accepted.

ELEVEN

"Have you heard of the game Fuck, Marry, Kill?" asked Alice.

"Sure," said Nate, who was feeling almost completely numb at this point. "Somebody gives you three celebrities, and you choose which one you would fuck, which one you would marry, and which one you would kill."

"Right. My sister and I were at this party filled with rich assholes, and one of the rich assholes suggested that we play. So we went around this gigantic living room, maybe thirty of us, and somebody would name three celebrities, and they'd point to somebody else and make them put them into the three categories. It was going fine at first. They'd fuck Ryan Reynolds, marry Harrison Ford, and kill Timothy Olyphant. Not how I'd arrange it, but you know what I mean. Then somebody, not me, was trying to be cute and named three people in the room. And so it went in that direction."

"Okay," said Nate. He decided not to think about this. He'd just

"Other people had said they'd kill Renee. She's the one who was hosting the party, she and her new husband. She laughed about it. It was all in good fun. Nobody was taking it seriously or personally. The wine was flowing, and people started cheating. So they'd add whatever names they wanted. When I got called on, I said I'd kill Renee—which, again, I wasn't the first, and she was one of the names given to me. Then I added my own names. I said I'd fuck her husband and marry her ex-boyfriend, who was at the party. Her husband didn't know they'd been a couple, or I'm sure her ex never would have been there. Everybody laughed and we moved on, but Renee...she didn't think it was very amusing."

ALICE AND CINDY SAT SIDE-BY-SIDE ON WOODEN CHAIRS. ALICE could still hear Olympia and Peter crying, although the sounds of her children grew quieter and quieter as they were led away.

"Please, give me my kids back," said Alice. "They didn't do anything."

"I know," said the man in the facemask. "This is all about you. So, Alice, I hear you like to play games."

Alice shook her head. "I hate games."

"Then I guess I've been misinformed. Oh well. What you're going to do is play a very special game of Fuck, Marry, Kill. You will be given three eligible bachelors, and you will choose which one you would like to fuck, which one you would like to marry, and which one you would like to kill. After you've made your decision, you will have exactly thirty days to fuck, marry, and kill your selections."

"Are you—?"

"If you're asking if I'm serious, yes. If you're asking if I'm out of my mind, no. This is very much for real. If, at the end of thirty days, you have not completed the game, your children will be killed. Not tortured—a quick and painless death from a bullet to the head. But still, dead kids. Do I need to explain this again?"

"No," said Alice. "You don't."

"Good. Now, you may think this is all one big joke. It sounds too over-the-top to be true, right? I get it." The man took out a gun and pressed the barrel against Cindy's forehead. "So my job is to dissuade you of the idea that this might be a joke."

NATE WAS HAVING INTENSE DIFFICULTY PROCESSING WHAT HE WAS hearing. "You wanted us to get married...because you're playing a game of Fuck, Marry, Kill?"

"Yes," said Alice. "That is exactly what I'm telling you. I lied, I was manipulative, I promised you this sexual paradise, and it was to save the lives of my children."

"I don't even know what to say."

"I don't expect you to be articulate right now."

Nate couldn't figure out his own emotional state. Was he angry? Was he devastated? Did he think she was full of shit? Was he terrified for the safety of her children? His mind was a maelstrom.

He opened his mouth, couldn't think of what to say, and closed it again.

"I know this doesn't mean anything right now," said Alice. "But a lot of what I said to you was the truth. I really, really like you. I loved spending time with you. I laughed at your jokes for real. I would never actually agree to an open relationship, but the sex was great. Would I have married you this quickly if we met under normal circumstances? No, of course not. Would I have wanted to be your girlfriend? Yes. Would we have gotten married eventually? Maybe. The feelings were real, even if my motives were a lie."

"You're right," said Nate. "That doesn't mean anything right now."

"Fair enough."

"YOUR CHILDREN WILL HAVE A NANNY," SAID THE MAN. "THEY'LL receive three meals a day, and their nutritional needs will be met. They'll have plenty of enrichment activities. Their nanny will do everything she can to make sure they're not too scared. Every once in a while, when we know you're alone, we'll call and let you briefly speak with them. As long as you don't break the rules, you have no need to worry about their safety during the thirty days of the game. If something terrible happens to them, it's your fault, not ours."

"I understand," said Alice.

"Good. Then come with me."

He walked her to a table, upon which rested three large glossy photographs.

"I don't know any of these guys," said Alice.

"You're not supposed to."

"There's nothing to go by. Just their faces."

"Correct."

"That's not how the game works. It's not supposed to be anonymous faces. The idea is that you know something about them. That's the whole point."

"I agree," said the man. "But I think we can also agree the game is usually completely hypothetical. Once we've added the twist that you're going to actually go out and do these things or else your children will die, it's okay to tweak the rest of the format as well."

"So it doesn't even matter who I pick."

"Well, it *does*, because these are real people. I will promise you there are no curveballs. None of these men are already married or gay."

Alice hesitated. "Fine," she said, tapping one of the pictures. "He looks like the sluttiest one. Him for Fuck."

"Dirk Maynard. His contact information is on the back of the picture. He frequents clubs looking for action, so you chose well. Next?"

She studied the pictures for a moment. "He has kind eyes. Him for Marry."

"Nathan Sommer. Restaurant server. Seems to be a relatively decent human being, so another wise choice. And that leaves Shane Flagler."

"He looks the most like an asshole."

The man smiled. "No, Dirk Maynard is the asshole."

"But you said I chose well."

"I was going to say that about whomever you picked." The man slid the pictures together and handed them to her. "Here you go. Fuck, Marry, Kill. Best of luck to you."

"Am I the first one?" Nate asked.

"No. Fuck was the easiest one, obviously. I started there. You were the second."

"Which leaves—"

"Kill. I have one week to do it."

"You're going to kill someone?"

"Yeah," said Alice. "I am."

"You really mean that? You're seriously planning to kill somebody?"

"I have to. I believe them, Nate. I believe without a shred of doubt that they will follow through on their threat to execute my babies. So I'm going to finish the game."

"But it's murder." Nate felt like an absolute idiot after he said it. Alice did, in fact, know that she was talking about the act of murder. Right now his brain felt like it was bouncing around in his head, and it was extremely difficult to think of something intelligent to say.

To her credit, Alice did not call him a dumbass. She seemed to understand that his mental health was not at its best right now.

"I have to do it," she said. "They're forcing me to choose between the lives of my children and a stranger, and I'm choosing my children."

"What if you get caught? What if you go to prison?"

"My anxiety level is through the roof because of those questions. I'm going to try to plan it out carefully enough that I don't get caught."

"There has to be another way."

"I wish there was."

"You really don't think you should call the police?"

"I *really* don't think I should call the police. They were very clear about what would happen if I did."

"But…maybe they wouldn't kill them if they knew the FBI was on the way. It would be way better for them to get convicted of kidnapping instead of murder, right?"

"Renee wouldn't do something like this if all I had to do was point her out to the cops. Her husband has deep pockets. He's covered his tracks. All I would do is get my kids killed."

"Are you sure?"

"No, I'm not sure. I don't need to be sure. I'm not taking the risk."

"Who do you have to kill?"

"I'm not ready to give you a name yet."

Nate didn't want to think about the murder anymore. "How do we get an annulment? Do we go back to the chapel? Should we go now?"

"Absolutely not. We can't just turn around and cancel the marriage."

"Oh, the hell with that. We got married under false pretenses. You can't expect me to keep going along with it."

"I just need you to go along with it until I've won the game," said Alice. "We can get an annulment after I've got Olympia and Peter back."

"What if it's a narrow window of opportunity? What if we only have, like, seventy-two hours?"

"It'll be okay. You'll tell them I lied about having kids and being sick. You're not stuck with me, I promise. But I really need your help."

"With what?"

Alice sat down next to him. "I know that I've sent your life into a tailspin. I completely get it if you're in a daze right now. But I'm going to need you to snap out of it, as much as you possibly can. When you ask a question like, 'With what?' it makes me worry you aren't understanding the things I'm telling you."

"No, I understand," said Nate. "You need me to help you kill a guy."

"That's right."

"I can't murder anybody."

"Even if I asked you to, that would be against the rules. I just need you to help me. Talk it out and see if I've overlooked anything. Help me get rid of the body afterward."

"You want me to be an accomplice?"

"Yes."

"And risk spending the rest of my life in prison?"

"I'm confident that if we work together, we can do it without getting caught."

"You're confident, huh?"

"We make a great team," said Alice.

"Oh, sure, we make a fantastic team! You lied to me about everything, but by golly, we're the best team there is! Do you know the most important element in a teammate? One thing that towers above everything else? Do you, Alice? Do you know what that element is?"

"Enlighten me."

"It's fucking *trust!* And, hey, you may not have noticed, but you've made it just a wee bit difficult to trust you right now. To refresh your memory, it was that whole thing where you tricked me into marrying you. Happened not all that long ago. We can go for a walk, and I can point out the chapel for you, if you want."

"Nate, stop. Close your eyes, take some deep breaths, count to ten, and then we'll resume this."

"I'm fine without counting to ten, thanks."

"It could be worse. You could've been Kill."

"Yeah, I could also have been Fuck! That guy sure lucked out, huh? Why aren't you asking Mr. Fuck to help you commit premeditated murder?"

"Because he was an idiot, and he could barely fuck me," said Alice. "There was no connection between us. With you, and I know you don't believe me, I truly think the connection is real."

"And because of our super-strong magical soulmate connection, you want me to help you kill somebody?"

"I'd like to think you still care enough about me to want to help."

"So I can have an innocent man's death on my conscience?"

"How will your conscience feel if my children die? Do you care more about this random man than my kids? I wish you could meet them. If you could see us together, you'd understand. If you had kids of your own, you'd understand. The first time you hold that baby in your arms, you know what it feels like to have a piece of your heart outside your body. You know what it feels like to love another person unconditionally, without restraint. And you'll make a vow, then and there, to protect that baby from the world. No matter what."

"How do I know you're telling the truth now?" asked Nate. "How do I know you aren't just using me to help kill one of your enemies?"

Alice let out a frustrated sigh. "Why would we need to get married for you to help me kill somebody?"

"Because I couldn't be compelled to testify against you."

"Shit. You're right. That's a good reason. I literally hadn't thought of that." She sighed again. "If you think I fabricated this entire thing, where I lied to you about almost everything to get you to marry me, then confessed the lies to get you to help me commit a murder, I may not be able to change your mind. I wish I hadn't told you."

"I wish you hadn't told me, either. I would *love* to be living in ignorant bliss right now."

"Sorry."

"Oh, don't give it another thought. It's perfectly fine."

Nate knew he was being a jerk, but he couldn't think of another time in his life where he was more justified in behaving like one. He felt like a complete idiot. How could he not have seen this coming? Not the whole "She's playing a game of Fuck, Marry, Kill," of course, but the idea that she had some kind of ulterior motive? Why had he believed her when she said she was dying?

Because she'd been damned convincing. She'd faked an X-Ray...not that faking an X-Ray would be difficult at all, he supposed.

She was damned convincing now.

He believed her.

Maybe he was still being a complete and total dumbass, but, yes, he believed that she was in this deranged game and that she was doing all of this to rescue her children.

Which meant she fully intended to move on to Kill.

"What do you want to know about Olympia and Peter?" asked Alice. "Ask me anything."

"It's fine," he said.

"Seriously. Anything you want to know. Ask me."

He knew what she was doing. She was trying to make him more connected to her children and also convince him she was telling the truth. Challenging him to stump her. Test how thoroughly she'd worked out the backstory of her potentially fictional offspring.

"There's no need for this. I believe you." Nate couldn't help but smile. "Wow. I have stepchildren. At least temporarily."

Alice burst into tears.

"No, no...I meant because of the annulment, not because of... that's not what I meant." He put his arms around her and gave her a tight hug. She pressed her face into his chest.

As messed up as this whole situation was, it still felt right to be this close to her.

He held her for a couple of minutes until she stopped crying. She pulled away and wiped her eyes. "I'm sorry."

"Don't be."

"I kept going back and forth on whether I should tell you or not. The rules said I could. But it meant dragging you even further into this. I just...I just don't want to do this, this horrible thing, and then have my babies raised by their dad anyway because I'm locked away."

"Does he know they're missing?"

"No. This is the first time I've been happy that he's a shitty father. He thinks they're at summer camp. So does everybody else. I have no idea how I'd explain this during the school year."

"And your sister?"

"They handled that. She took a leave of absence and is back-packing in Europe. Finding herself."

"What about a paper trail? Wouldn't she be using credit cards?"

"That is something I'll be dealing with when she, quote unquote, doesn't return from her trip. The man in the facemask explained that I have much more important things to worry about."

"Were you close?"

"Yeah."

"I'm sorry."

"I can't wait for this game to be over so I can let out all my grief," said Alice. "Right now I'm being a soldier. A fucking robot."

Nate tried to think of something he could say to console her, but came up completely blank. After struggling for a moment, he landed on, "I'm sure you'll get your kids back."

Alice nodded. "I intend to."

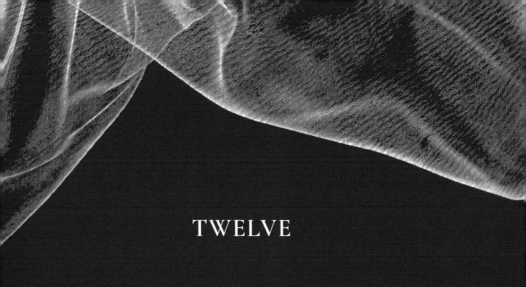

TWELVE

"What now?" asked Nate.

"I guess now you have a really important decision to make," said Alice. "I told you all of this because I wanted you to help me, and because I didn't think I could keep up the charade of being a happy wife while I was planning a murder. I wanted to tell you on my own terms, instead of you demanding to know what was wrong. So, I just need to know: Will you help me?"

Nate genuinely cared about her. He didn't want to see any harm come to her children. But helping her kill somebody? Or simply *letting* her kill somebody? He didn't think he could do that.

"I don't know," Nate admitted.

"I guess it was never going to be an easy decision."

"I need some time to think about it. Not a ton of time. I know there's a ticking clock. Just let me go for a walk."

"That's a good idea," said Alice. "Let's take a walk."

"I meant by myself. So I could think."

"I won't say a word." Alice crossed her heart. "Not a single word. I won't speak unless spoken to, I promise."

"You think I'll run to the cops."

"I don't know what you'll do. I'm not sure you even know what you'll do."

Nailed it. Nate didn't have a clue. All he knew was that he couldn't make an intelligent decision if he was standing here being emotionally manipulated. He needed to get away from Alice, wander the streets of Vegas for a while, and figure this out.

"You're asking me for an unbelievable amount of trust," Nate told her. "So you need to trust me in return."

"You expect me to trust, on the lives of my children, that you won't call the police?"

"What do the rules say? You can't call the cops, but can I?"

"You're bound by the same rules. They obviously didn't leave open a loophole where you're allowed to report the kidnapping."

"Well, it would've been stupid not to ask, right?"

"Right. It's fine. I wasn't being a bitch."

"So let me walk for a while. I promise I won't do anything but walk and think."

"I'm staking my children's lives on your promise."

"And I appreciate that."

"I can't do it."

"Are you saying that I'm not free to leave? What are you going to do if I just walk to the door, attack me?"

"It's not like that, Nate. You understand where I'm coming from, right?"

"I do. But we need to trust each other."

"I trust you. But even though we're married, we've only known each other for three weeks." Alice didn't smile, but Nate got the sense she was trying to create a moment of levity.

"Okay," said Nate. "You're right. It's asking too much." He didn't really believe that, but he'd let her win for now. He reached into his pocket, took out his cell phone, and placed it on the desk. "I'm going to leave my phone here. I give you permission to follow me. I don't want to feel you breathing down my neck, but you can be close enough to stop me if I ask to borrow somebody's phone."

"And if you start talking to a cop?"

"Then I'm going to tell them that in order to get your kidnapped children back, you're going to murder an innocent man as part of a deranged game of Fuck, Marry, Kill, and you'll rush over there and apologize on behalf of your drunk husband. I won't talk to the police. I swear to God I won't. All I need is to be able to think, and I can't be analytical enough if you're near me."

"All right," said Alice. "I'm going to trust you."

"Then let's go for a walk."

NATE WAS TELLING THE TRUTH. HE HAD NO INTENTION OF contacting the police.

Not tonight, anyway.

It was *very* difficult for him to imagine a scenario in which he helped Alice. Would he have to dismember a corpse? Bury somebody in a shallow grave? Canoe out to the middle of a pond and sink the body? That was all unthinkable.

He felt horrible about Alice's plight. Truly awful. His heart ached for what she was going through. But was he willing to spend the rest of his life behind bars to help her get her kids back? No. He wasn't sure if that made him intelligent and rational, or selfish and evil, but he was not going to prison just because she pissed off some rich psychotic frenemy. It simply was not going to happen.

So what *was* he going to do?

How could he help her, without...*helping* her?

Just how closely were they monitoring her? Yes, they had the necklace, and, yes, it still kind of mortified him that perverts had watched and listened to him having sex with her. But surely it wasn't this generously funded global operation that was able to spy on their every move. Maybe they were tracking his phone, but if he was walking down this crowded street in Las Vegas and happened to whisper something to a stranger, would they really know?

Almost certainly not.

The key word, of course, was "almost." It was like the risk of a random IRS audit. They probably weren't going to catch you, but if they *did*...

The paranoia that they might be listening or watching at any given time was probably enough to keep Alice from breaking the rules. She might have been able to whisper something into his ear while they were taking a shower together, but what if the microphone in the necklace did pick it up?

Honestly, the whole "We're watching your every move" thing was probably a bluff. But if it wasn't, or they happened to be watching at the moment he tried something, he could get her kids killed. And if he was responsible for the deaths of her children, he'd have some big-time self-loathing to cope with.

So for the sake of Alice and her children—if they were real— Nate was going to proceed as if somebody was watching his every move and hearing his every word.

They returned to the hotel room. "There's no other way out of this?" Nate asked. "You can't reason with them?"

Alice shook her head. "Based on what I've told you, do they sound like you can reason with them?"

"I guess not." Nate didn't really believe that. Maybe Alice couldn't reason with them, but a lot of Nate's restaurant customers left big tips. He knew how to charm people. Perhaps it could be as simple as having a productive conversation. "Have you worked out a plan to kill the guy yet?"

"I've followed him. The truth is, if I failed with you, it didn't matter anyway. 'Kill' is the one that will haunt me. I had to do the other two first, or else I might have a murder on my conscience *and* dead children."

That made sense. "But you know how you're going to do it?"

"I have an idea. He lives in a big apartment complex. Lots of neighbors. I think he works from home, because he's there most of the day. I was going to strike up a conversation, make him think he's going to get lucky, and take him somewhere isolated."

"Then shoot him?"

"Probably stab him."

"That works."

"Obviously, I can't buy a registered gun I'm going to use as a murder weapon," said Alice. "I have no idea where I'd get an untraceable gun. Do you?"

"Not a clue."

"I'd love to have you there in case something goes wrong."

"Like what?"

"Like the million things that could go wrong when you lure somebody into the woods to murder them."

"So…tackle him if he escapes?"

"That's one possibility. But to be clear, it's going to be very carefully planned, and I'm not going to take any chances. I don't expect you to have to do anything but be there. I won't ask you to do anything violent. When we bury him, I'll do all of the digging. I just want you there as an extra layer of protection."

"I'm still an accomplice, though."

Alice lowered her eyes. "Yes. You are."

"Let me be completely honest," said Nate. "I'm not vowing to help you to the very end, no matter what. I have no intention of going to prison. I'll do what I can, but I'm also reserving the right to bail at any time, no questions asked."

Alice nodded. "That's fair."

"I mean it."

"I understand."

"And you're going to record a confession. You can be vague about why you're doing this, but you're going to say that you blackmailed me, or something like that. You lied to get me to marry you, then you blackmailed me into helping you." A confession like this wouldn't be a "get out of jail free" card for Nate, but at least it would be *something*.

Alice hesitated. "Okay, but you have to promise not to share it unless the walls are truly closing in. You're my husband. If I become a suspect, they'll ask you some questions. I'm putting you in a terrible position, and I one hundred percent understand your need to protect yourself, but I don't want you to panic and play them a confession video prematurely."

"I'll wait until the walls are closing in," Nate assured her. Maybe that was the truth.

"All right." Alice smiled. "I think we're gaining back some trust."

Nate shrugged. "What now?"

"Get some sleep."

"Sure you don't want to have kinky sex in front of the perverts watching us?"

"I felt sick about that," said Alice. "But I was trying to get you to marry me. I thought it was a good tactic."

"It was," Nate admitted.

"Maybe when this is over, we'll revisit it."

"Don't do that."

"Do what?"

"You're back to being manipulative. We're not going to have sex when this is over. We're not going to stay a married couple, or be boyfriend and girlfriend, or whatever. I hope you get your kids back. I really do. But when you're reunited with them, we're going to keep in touch for as long as it takes to get the annulment, and that's the end."

"Right," said Alice. "Of course."

She seemed genuinely hurt. Nate felt a tinge of remorse and then immediately felt ridiculous about it. She was doing what she needed to do to save her children. Fine. But if she thought their relationship was going to continue after this, she was out of her damn mind.

And he didn't think she was out of her mind. She was trying to keep him on her side with the promise that, sexually, it would be worth his while. He believed her story and would help her within reason, but when this was all sorted out, they were *done*.

"Yeah, let's get some sleep," he said, though he expected to lie awake with thoughts rocketing through his brain until it was time to get up and go to the airport.

"I'll call the front desk and have them send up a cot," said Alice. "For me, not you."

"That's not necessary. We can sleep in the same bed."

"Are you sure?"

"Yeah," said Nate. "There's no reason to make this more unpleasant than it needs to be. I'm pissed, but I'm not going to be antagonistic."

"Thank you."

Alice went into the bathroom. Nate lay on the bed, wondering yet again if helping her would be the stupidest thing he'd ever do in his life, second only to mouthing off to Mad Dog Mitch during his inevitable upcoming prison stint. He didn't owe her anything.

Nate wavered back and forth on the issue until Alice emerged, wearing dark blue pajamas that hid all her curves. Had they been packed specifically because she knew there'd be no seduction tonight?

Nate continued wavering back and forth during his own shower.

He may not owe her anything, but he couldn't *not* help her.

That said, if there was any hint that the plan was going sideways, he'd bail in a heartbeat.

After drying off and putting on his own unsexy pajamas, Nate climbed into bed, leaving plenty of space between him and his new wife. Not how he'd expected his wedding night to go.

"What if I talked to her?" he asked.

"Who?"

"The lady who did this."

Alice vigorously shook her head. "No. Absolutely not."

"Is it against the rules? Did they specifically say that you aren't allowed to speak with her?"

"No. But what would you even say?"

"I'd try to reason with her. Smooth things over."

"You don't even know her."

"Right, but I know *you*—well, excluding all of the lies—and I'm pretty persuasive when I want to be. Maybe I could turn on my maximum charm. It's worth a shot, isn't it?"

"You could make things worse," said Alice.

"I'd be on my best behavior."

"No. I desperately need your help, Nate, and you'll never know how much I appreciate you, but don't do anything unless I say it's okay."

Nate nodded. "All right. Goodnight."

Alice was asleep within a few minutes, softly snoring. Nate wondered how she could fall asleep so quickly, considering the circumstances. Then it occurred to him that things were easier for her now. She'd gotten him to marry her. She was one great big step closer to getting her kids back. Of course she'd be more at peace.

It took him much longer to fall asleep, but finally he did.

When he woke up, he was spooning Alice. It felt right.

He immediately rolled over and apologized.

"It's okay," she told him. Moments later she was snoring again.

Nate glanced over at the clock. 5:13 AM.

He lay there, trying and failing to go back to sleep.

He'd told Alice that he wouldn't do anything without her approval. But she was going to *murder* somebody. Wouldn't it be better to try to talk this out with the people who were doing this to her?

Clearly, her ex-friend wasn't entirely sane, but was she completely unreasonable?

Maybe Nate could work out a deal.

He was going to try.

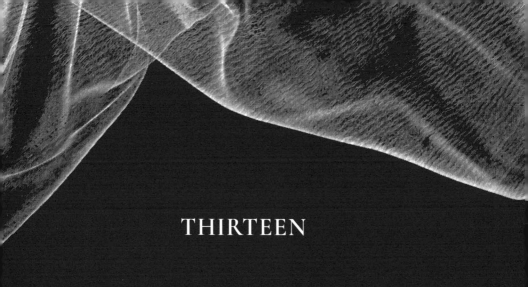

THIRTEEN

In the morning, Nate and Alice got up and packed. They were cordial with each other, but there was no playful banter, and they certainly didn't behave like a new husband and wife. They didn't really speak on the ride to the airport, and Alice slept during most of the flight.

Nate still thought that diplomacy was the best solution to the problem.

As they walked toward baggage claim in the Atlanta airport, Nate said, "Are we going back to our own places?"

"I'd rather stay with you," said Alice. "It's not even my place. I rented a house so I wouldn't have to hide all of the evidence of my children's existence from you. I figured it would be a lot harder to convince you to marry me if you thought I had two young kids."

"I need some time to decompress. I didn't sleep worth shit last night. Let's just go our separate ways and detox."

"Detox, huh?" said Alice.

"Did that offend you? Because I don't apologize if it did."

"No, no, it's fine. I get it. When are we going to get back together?"

"I have to work tomorrow, but it's the early shift. I'll be off at six-thirty. How about I go straight from work to your place, and then we can have a very long and serious talk about the next step?"

"Okay. That's reasonable. I just don't want to waste time, you know?"

"I know. But I also won't be any good to you if I can't focus. Tomorrow evening, I promise."

AS NATE ENTERED HIS APARTMENT AND PUT DOWN HIS SUITCASE, HE wondered how heavily his apartment was being monitored. Could they see and hear everything he was doing? Or was it all bullshit, and they weren't spying on him at all?

He was exhausted, but he wanted to get started, so he decided to go with his old standby, the coffee nap. If you gulped down a cup of coffee and then napped for twenty-five minutes, the caffeine would get into your system really quickly.

Twenty-five minutes later, he was ready to go.

Alice would be enraged with him. Yet Nate, who had plenty of experience winning over difficult people, was very confident in his ability to not completely mess this up. Why not try to talk this out? As long as he didn't break any of their rules, what was the worst that could happen?

He just had to figure out who to speak with.

He wasn't sure if Alice even remembered that she'd said her frenemy's name: Renee.

Of course, there were probably hundreds of women named Renee in Atlanta, but how many of them were recently married? Even if the answer was "more than one," how many were recently married to a successful businessman with shady ties? Nate didn't think he'd need to hire a top-notch private investigator to solve this mystery—a few minutes on the Internet should do the trick.

As he typed, he wondered if they were monitoring his Internet search.

Didn't matter. He wasn't contacting the police.

It was very easy. Renee Landis had married Bryan Alec Walker a few months ago. Renee looked about Alice's age, while Walker looked like he was in his fifties. He looked more like a military drill sergeant than a mob boss, but even in this black-and-white picture, he had a gaze that made it easy to believe he'd ordered the occasional pair of cement shoes.

These were the right people. And their address was right there in the wedding announcement. He could be there in twenty minutes.

He took a shower so his aroma wouldn't negatively impact the negotiation, and stared inside his closet for a moment. What was the appropriate attire for trying to talk somebody into releasing kidnapped children? He settled on jeans and a nice button-down dark green shirt, the sort of thing he'd wear on a first date.

Nate glanced at himself in the mirror. He looked trustworthy and sincere.

What if he messed this up?

He wouldn't.

They might not be receptive to his efforts to just talk this whole thing out like mature adults, but they wouldn't kill the kids. Worst case scenario, they'd tell him to go fuck himself, and Alice would still have to commit murder. No worse off than before.

He got more and more nervous as he drove toward their home, but he knew he was doing the right thing.

The house wasn't quite a mansion, but it was *damn* nice. He pulled up to the front gate, rolled down his window, and pressed the button on the intercom.

"Yes?" a woman's voice asked.

"My name is Nathan Sommer. Here to see Renee Landis-Walker."

"Do you have an appointment?"

"No, I'm sorry."

There was a moment of silence. Then the gates slowly opened, and Nate drove through. He felt a little queasy watching the gates close behind him in the rearview mirror, even though there was nothing objectively sinister about that.

He parked next to a black Mercedes. He didn't mind his shitty vehicle, which reliably took him where he needed to go, but there was a vast chasm between the quality of these two automobiles. He walked to the front door and rang the doorbell. It was a couple of minutes before the door opened.

"Yes?" asked Renee. She was wearing a red cocktail dress. Nate wondered if she was going out, or if this was how rich people dressed when they were at home. Or maybe she'd changed for their meeting.

"Are you Renee Landis-Walker?"

"Yes."

"Like I said, I'm Nathan Sommer. You might know me."

"I don't." Nate wasn't sure if she was lying or not. He also couldn't tell if she was scowling at him, or if she simply had an extreme case of resting bitch face.

"May I come in?"

"It might be helpful to know what you want first."

"I want to talk about our mutual friend."

"Are you planning to name her, or do you just want me to guess?"

"Alice Vinestalk."

Renee smirked. "Alice, huh? 'Friend' is a very interesting word choice."

"Ex-friend, then. But you know who I'm talking about, right?"

"Yeah."

"But you don't know who I am?"

"Nope."

Nate suddenly wondered if Alice could've made up this entire thing. But, no, he didn't believe Renee. She knew exactly who he was.

"That's fine," he said. "I'm here because I'd like to try to work out a peace agreement between you two."

"Peace agreement? Are you fuckin' NATO?"

"I want to smooth things over. Come to an understanding."

"Good luck with that. Did she send you?"

"No. She has no idea I'm here."

"Interesting."

"Is your husband home?"

"Why? Planning to rape me if he isn't?"

"What? No!" Nate took a step back away from her. "I just think he should be included in this conversation."

"He's not home," said Renee. "But I'm not alone in the house. I could have somebody here in three seconds."

"That's not *at all* what I meant by my question."

"I'm sure it wasn't. Yeah, you can come in. Don't expect me to offer you a drink."

He followed her into the very large, luxurious living room. She sat down on a brown leather couch. When she didn't offer him a seat, he awkwardly chose the rocking chair across from her.

"I don't expect you two to reconcile," said Nate. "I'd just like to talk about what we can do to tone down the more extreme parts of your falling out."

"Are you fucking her?"

"We got married yesterday."

"That wasn't my question."

Nate wondered if this was an honesty test. "We've been intimate, yes."

Renee snickered. "*Intimate.*"

"It's not really relevant."

"It's relevant because I thought you might want to know that you're fucking a whore. She banged my boyfriend, and I guarantee she'll cheat on you. Hope you've had your shots, because she's going to bring some nasty shit home to your bed, if she hasn't already."

"I'm not here to talk about our marriage," said Nate. "I'm here to talk about you two. Seriously, Renee, there has to be a way we can talk this out like adults."

"I don't like it when you use my name."

"What do you want from her?"

"Why is it any of your concern?"

"Because she's my wife."

"Congratulations. Where's your gift registry, Dollar Tree? Would you like some fancy paper plates?"

Nate gave her a friendly smile. "That would be lovely. I prefer the coated kind where stuff doesn't soak through."

"Oh, I'm sorry," said Renee. "You thought we were being playful. That's my fault."

"I just don't like seeing your friendship fall apart because of a misunderstanding."

"There was no misunderstanding."

"She regrets what happened."

"I'm sure she does."

"I'm not saying that you should become besties. I just believe that there has to be a way to scale the feud back, so there aren't any winners or losers. Work with me. Tell me what we can do. Let's figure this out."

"I'm perfectly happy with the way things are going."

"Fine. You hate Alice. That's your choice, and I'm not going to tell you you're wrong. But there are other people involved. Why drag them into this?"

"What other people? You?"

"You know who I mean."

"Do I?"

"Her children."

"What about her children?"

"C'mon, are you going to make me come out and say it?"

"I'm not making you do anything."

"How can I convince you to let her children go?"

Renee smiled. She spoke very calmly. "What a perplexing thing to say. Are you mentally ill, Nathan? Did I let a crazy person into my house? Am I in danger right now?"

"No."

"I have no idea what you're talking about. I assumed Alice was home with her children right now. They're adorable—clearly they take after her ex-husband. But let me make sure I understand you correctly. Are you accusing me of kidnapping Alice's kids?"

"I'm not accusing you of anything."

"Good. I don't like to be falsely accused of things. It makes me and my husband very angry."

"I'd just like to discuss a way to work this out."

"Do you mean pay me?"

"If that's what it takes."

"How does a million dollars sound?"

"You know she doesn't have that."

"Right. And I don't think she could raise it no matter how much she whores herself out. So I guess there's no reason to keep discussing a financial angle, especially because I have no idea what the hell you're talking about. How do you think our talk is going so far?"

"There's room for improvement."

Renee nodded. "I agree."

"What about an apology? A truly sincere, groveling apology?"

"I would enjoy that."

"Really?"

"It wouldn't change anything, but I'd enjoy it."

"I know for a fact that she feels terrible about what happened."

"I'm glad to hear it. I very much doubt that she feels terrible about what she did to me."

"She does."

"I've known her a lot longer than you. I've known her since she had her mommy pick her up from a slumber party because she wet the bed. She might *regret* what she did to me, but she doesn't feel guilty about it. She cares about the consequences."

"Don't you think the consequences are a little over the top?"

Renee shrugged. "Regardless of what you're babbling about, the consequence I'm talking about is me cutting her out of my life. And I think she deserves everything that's happening to her."

"Let's be reasonable."

"I'm not a fan of you inviting yourself into my home and then calling me unreasonable. It's very rude. It honestly makes me kind of mad."

"Then I apologize," said Nate.

"Let me put you out of your misery. It's cute that you thought you could help. But showing up here accomplished absolutely nothing. It literally didn't change a thing. You would have accomplished more by staying home and masturbating in your apartment. So what I'd like you to do now is get the fuck out of my house before my husband comes home, because he's prone to fits of jealous rage, and I'd prefer that he not find us together. Is that okay with you?"

"I'd really like to talk to him, if you don't mind."

"I do mind. I want you to go. If you don't, I'll have to call the police. Do you want to talk to the police, Nathan? Can you think of anything bad that might happen if you talk to the police? Think carefully."

Nate stood up. The chair squeaked as it rocked back and forth. "Sorry for bothering you."

"It's all right. Sorry if this made you feel impotent."

Nate left, face burning. He wondered if he'd screwed this up, or if he'd simply walked into a no-win situation. He supposed it had been really naive to believe he could reason with the kind of psychopath who would do this sort of thing.

As he walked out the front door, he saw a man standing by his car. The man was dressed entirely in black, including his facemask.

"Uh, hi," Nate said.

The man waved him over. "C'mon. It's okay."

Shit. What should he do? Go back inside?

The man beckoned again. "Don't just stand there. You're finished with your business inside, right? Come on over. I'll open your car door for you."

"I don't want any trouble."

"Then the feeling is mutual. Please come over here, Nate. You prefer Nate to Nathan, right?"

"Either one is fine."

"Come over here."

Nate hesitated.

"Do you know what's happening now?" asked the man.

"What?"

"You're pissing me off. Because I'm standing here like an idiot waiting for you. Right now you're trespassing, which means I have the right to defend my employer's property. I would prefer not to shoot you in the head. And that preference is about cleanup, not conscience."

Nate didn't know if this was the same guy Alice had interacted with, but if so, he'd shot her sister right in front of her. There was no choice. Nate walked over to him.

"How'd your talk go?" the man asked. "Not well, I'll bet."

"Could've gone better."

"Here's what's going to happen. I have a billy club under my shirt. Despite what you see in the movies, it's extremely difficult to knock somebody unconscious, and I don't want to give you brain damage. So I'm going to beat the shit out of you until I feel like you're sufficiently incapacitated enough not to give me trouble."

"I won't give you any trouble," Nate promised.

"Glad to hear it. But I have a high-pressure job, and sometimes I just need to blow off a little steam." He reached under his shirt and took out the club. "If you get on the ground now, you're less likely to hurt yourself by falling on the cement."

"You don't have to do this."

"I know. I just explained why I want to. Try to keep up."

The man bashed Nate on the side of the head. Nate cried out and fell to his knees.

As the man hit him over and over, Nate retained consciousness, but things definitely got blurry.

FOURTEEN

Nate didn't resist as he was eased into the trunk of his own car. He had no memory of the man taking his keys. He was pretty sure he blacked out a few times during the drive.

When the lid of the trunk opened, the man helped him out, but let him fall onto the cement floor. "You can walk or crawl, doesn't matter to me," the man informed him.

Nate got up. The man led him over to a chair and shoved him down onto it.

"I don't feel like tying you up," said the man. "Are you going to behave?"

Nate nodded.

"Good. How's your head feeling? I tried not to hit you too hard."

"It hurts."

"It's supposed to hurt. Can you see clearly? Can you understand

The man punched him in the face. "What about now? Still with me?"

"Yeah."

"Good, good. Let's talk. Question for you. Let's say you walk by a sign that says, *'Please Don't Walk on the Grass.'* So instead, you ride your skateboard over it. You have technically followed the instructions, but have you complied with their intent?"

Nate shrugged. "I don't know their intent. Maybe they didn't want me to get stung by ants."

The man raised his fist as if to punch him again, then lowered it. "I'll give you credit for that answer. But you understand what I'm getting at, right?"

Nate spat out some blood. "I understand what *you're* getting at, but in the real world the sign would say *'Keep Off the Grass,'* not *'Please Don't Walk on the Grass.'* So you picked a stupid fucking example. If you don't want me on the grass, tell me to stay off the grass."

"You're right," said the man. "It was a bad example. Picked it off the top of my head. What I'm trying to say is that you knew perfectly well it was not okay to come to Ms. Walker's home."

"I don't agree with that at all. This is a game, right? I followed the rules given to me. If you left something out, that's not my fault. You should have paid a little more attention to your game design."

The man raised his fist again. Started to lower it, then punched Nate in the face.

"When you play Monopoly, it's understood that you can't just grab another player's piece and put it in jail, even though that's not specifically stated in the rules."

"Not the same thing," said Nate. "The Monopoly rules tell you explicitly what you *are* allowed to do. Everybody understands that the pieces can only be moved in the way that is spelled out in the rules. Your game told me explicitly what I *wasn't* allowed to do. And that didn't include showing up at Renee's house."

"Think you're a lawyer?"

"Restaurant server."

"I already knew that. You argue with people who try to send their food back?"

Nate shook his head. "Customer is always right."

"Fine. Here's the deal, though. In this game, we have total control, and if I get pissed at you for trying to exploit a loophole, *I'm* always right. Do you want to have a game of your own? Do you?"

The adrenaline that had kept Nate going throughout this experience seemed to instantly vanish, leaving him sick to his stomach with terror. "No."

"You sure? I'd love to set one up."

"I don't want my own game."

"Alice has two children. Do you think she'd be any less compliant if it was only one? I could shoot the boy in the head, and the game would still go on as planned."

"Please don't do that," said Nate. "I'm sorry. I thought I was following the rules. I wasn't trying to cheat."

"I know. Your heart was in the right place even if your brain wasn't. We're going to call this a warning. A very, very serious warning. Do not try to come up with inventive solutions to Alice's problem. The only way she gets her kids back is to kill her target. Understand?"

"I understand," said Nate. "What now?"

"I'm going to hit you a few more times because I've got some frustration to vent, and I don't want to take it out on people I care about. Then I'm going to put you back in your trunk. Any questions?"

"Do you really have to hit me?"

The man nodded. "Yes, I do. Sorry."

"In the face?"

"Chest area, mostly. One good punch in the face."

"All right."

"Swallow the blood instead of spitting it out. I don't want to mop."

The beating was over quickly, ending when Nate fell out of the chair and onto the floor. Flecks of blood hit the cement—he hoped the man didn't notice.

"Are you going to get up and walk over to the trunk, or are you going to make me drag you?" the man asked. "There's a right answer, and there's a wrong answer. The wrong answer involves me twisting your arm until it breaks."

"You're weirdly chatty," said Nate.

"I don't have many people to talk to."

"I'll get up."

"Thanks. Appreciate it."

Nate got to his feet, fought off a dizzy spell, and started to walk.

"Wrong way," said the man.

Nate turned around and walked in the other direction.

"Let me help you." The man took Nate by the hand and led him over to his car. He helped him climb into the trunk, then slammed the lid shut. Nate lay in the darkness for a moment, then passed out.

He didn't wake up until the lid opened again.

"C'mon, buddy, you can do it," said the man, helping Nate out of the trunk. "You okay to drive? Not going to kill anybody on your way home?"

"I'm fine."

"If you start to feel dizzy, pull over. Don't go above the speed limit. Get home safe, okay?"

"Okay."

"And have fun explaining to your wife why you got your ass kicked." The man chuckled and handed Nate his keys. "You've been a good sport about this whole thing. Just remember that if we have to talk again, I'm either going to shoot you in the head or make your life hell on earth. Got it?"

"Got it."

"Good." The man opened the driver's side door, and Nate slowly got into his car, moving like a ninety-year-old and hurting with every breath. "Seatbelt."

Nate put on his seatbelt. He started the engine and drove away.

He had to stop twice to wait out a dizzy spell and once to vomit. But he made it home without claiming any innocent victims. He got a few concerned looks as he walked to his apartment, but assured the woman who offered to drive him to the hospital that he was perfectly all right.

He staggered into the bathroom and peed. The urine stream was pink, but not too bad.

He collapsed onto his bed, closed his eyes, and went to sleep.

NATE AWOKE TO THE SOUND OF SOMEBODY POUNDING ON HIS DOOR. He reluctantly got out of bed and walked toward the noise, pausing halfway there so he didn't topple over. When he opened it, Alice was standing out there.

"Oh, thank God," she said. Then her eyes widened with concern. "What happened?"

"Come in," he said, standing aside.

Alice walked into his apartment, and he shut the door.

"Are you okay?" Alice asked. "I called you a dozen times."

"Sorry. I slept through it."

She led him over to the couch and helped him sit down. "Can I get you anything?" Alice asked.

"I could use some water."

Alice got him a bottle of water from the refrigerator, then sat down next to him. Nate gulped down half of it, gasped for breath, then finished the rest.

"So what happened?" Alice asked. The tone of her voice was still one of concern, but there was a definite streak of irritation creeping into it.

Nate weighed his options. It would be easy to lie. Just say he got mugged. Three guys came out of nowhere, kicked his ass, and stole his mug wallet.

But he really didn't want to get caught in the lie. When Alice called to speak with her children, would the man in the facemask tell her what happened?

This was probably a time for honesty.

"I fucked up," he told her.

Alice immediately stiffened. "Why? What did you do?"

"I went to talk to Renee."

"Please tell me you're joking. Please fucking tell me you're joking."

Nate shook his head. "I thought we could have a pleasant conversation. I don't want you to have to murder somebody, and if I could talk everything out and get her to change her mind, shouldn't I at least try?"

"No, Nate. You should not at least try. I told you not to do it. I told you very clearly, very fucking clearly, not to go speak with Renee."

"I know."

Alice took a long, deep breath. "How did it go?"

"She...she wasn't receptive."

"What did she say?"

Honestly, Nate was having difficulty remembering the conversation. "She was kind of sarcastic. Kind of a bitch. She didn't actually admit to what she was doing, but she didn't try that hard to deny it. She basically just shut down the idea that she was going to call off the game."

"Okay," said Alice. Her face was contorted as if trying to hold in a scream. "And who beat you up?"

"A guy in a black facemask. I assume the same guy who killed your sister and told you the rules."

"Did he say anything to you while he was beating you up?"

"Never do this again, and if I do, I'll get my own game."

Alice closed her eyes for a few moments. A tear trickled down her cheek. Then she stood up.

"I could kill you right now," she said.

"I'm so sorry, Alice."

She slapped him across the face with such force, it felt like she was trying to take his head completely off. His jaw was already sore, and the blow sent a wave of pain down his entire body. He was surprised to be able to contain his reaction to a loud grunt instead of a scream.

She did it again and might as well have stabbed him in the face with a butcher knife. Nate flopped over on his side.

"You son of a bitch! You put my children at risk!"

"I know," Nate managed to say. "But everything's fine."

"How do you know that? How do you know they didn't execute them?"

Nate sat up, blinking away tears. "Because they would have told me. The guy in the mask wouldn't tell me to never do it again, let me go, and then kill your kids. I got off with a warning. It's fine."

Alice swung at him again, but Nate grabbed her arm before the blow could land. He deserved this, but he couldn't let her keep hitting him—it felt like his skin was going to split apart.

She tugged her arm away from him. "I trusted you. I *trusted* you, you piece of shit!"

"I did what I thought was right!"

"Do you really think you know better than me? You're a fucking pawn, Nate! The decision was not yours to make! You had no right to do that! My kids could be dead now, all because of you!"

"They're not, okay? I promise you, it's fine."

Alice punched him in the chest before he could block her. Though she certainly wasn't aiming with pinpoint precision, she got him right on a particularly tender bruise, and he cried out in pain.

"Stop it!" he shouted. "Just stop it!"

"I need your help! I can't have you making things worse!" She threw another punch, and he grabbed her by the wrist.

"Alice, I need you to stop this," said Nate, struggling to keep his voice as steady as possible. "I know you're furious. You deserve to be. But I'm not going to let you attack me, okay? You need to calm down."

To the best of Nate's knowledge, at no point in human history had telling a woman she needed to calm down had the desired effect. But he didn't know what else to say.

Alice tried to pull her wrist free. "Let go of me."

"I'll let go of you when you stop hitting me. My whole body is on fire. How am I supposed to help you get rid of a corpse if I can't even walk?"

Alice tried again to yank her wrist free, but Nate held it firm. "Let me go, or I'll scream," she said.

"Then scream. Let the police come to investigate a domestic disturbance. See how that works out."

"Goddamn you, Nate. I never should have told you."

Nate very much agreed. "But you did. You made me complicit.

So I'm not a pawn, I'm a…I don't know what kind of chess piece I am, but it's not a pawn."

Alice continued to try to pull her wrist away. "Let me go."

"If you try to hit me again, I won't hit you back, but I'll have to restrain you. Do you understand?"

Alice nodded. He let her go.

"You could have let me go on thinking you were sick, and that we had a happy marriage. But you didn't. You dragged me into this. And if I'm part of it, I get to help make decisions."

"You didn't help decide anything. You went off and did something stupid."

"And I've taken ownership for my mistake. It won't happen again. You can tell me I'm a piece of shit all you want, but I need you to stop being violent."

"Fine."

She stood up, stormed into the bathroom, and slammed the door shut. A moment later Nate heard her sobbing. He continued sitting on the bed for a few minutes, figuring that a knock on the door to ask if she was all right would not be welcomed.

She finally emerged, face red and blotchy.

"I forgive you," she said.

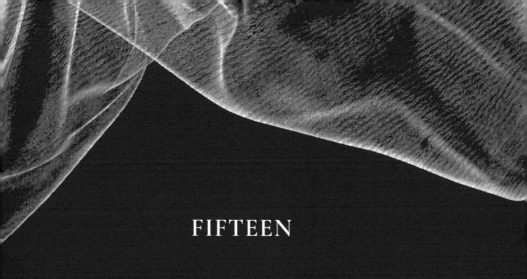

FIFTEEN

"I have a plan," Alice told Nate.

"I'm listening."

"I want to keep things as simple as possible. I'll try to seduce him. Let him drive me out to a secluded area. You'll be waiting there. I'll kill him. If things go sideways, you'll be there to help, but I have to be the one to do it. Then you'll help me dispose of the body and take care of whatever cleanup is necessary. I'll get my kids back. We'll get our marriage annulled, then go our separate ways."

"So, pretty much what you already told me we were going to do," said Nate. "Sounds nice and easy," said Nate.

"Please don't be sarcastic."

"I'm not. What could possibly go wrong?"

"You're still being sarcastic."

"You're right. I'm sorry. Is the plan still to do it with a knife?"

"Yes. I'm going to slash his throat."

"That'll do it."

"I'm going to take the seduction pretty far," said Alice. "I want his defenses to be completely down. He might even be inside me when I do it. Are you okay with that?"

"Do you really think my problem with this is the infidelity?"

"I'm just asking."

"No, Alice, I'm not going to be so consumed with fiery jealousy that I try to kill him myself."

"I want you to know what to expect. That's all."

"I'll be ready. Hopefully I don't get too turned on and start masturbating right there next to the car."

Alice was silent for a moment. "I know I went a little psycho, but I'd like to call a truce. No more yelling. No more sarcasm. Let's be kind and respectful to each other and discuss everything like we're a happily married couple. We're making this so much more unpleasant than it has to be."

Right, Nate thought. *We wouldn't want planning a murder to be unpleasant.* But he didn't want to make a sarcastic comment immediately after Alice called for a moratorium on sarcastic comments. "I can be nice if you can."

"Then let's do that."

"Okay. So where are you going to seduce him? His favorite bar?"

"I need to follow him and watch for the right moment. Do you know what a 'meet cute' is?"

"A what?"

"I think Roger Ebert coined the term. It's in a romantic comedy, when the lead characters first meet in a wacky and endearing way. So, for example, she spills lobster bisque all over his shirt."

"What movie is that from?"

"None. I just threw it out there. My thought is that I'll be carrying a birthday cake, and I'll accidentally bump into him and drop it. When he's helping me clean it up, I'll strike up a conversation. Or something like that. It doesn't specifically have to be cake."

"You think that'll work?"

Alice shrugged. "I'm not hideous, but I don't know his taste in women. His reaction might be, 'Bitch, watch where you're going.' He might be too smart to drive off with a woman he just met. I'll have to be flexible and adjust to whatever happens. But my hope is that I can crank up the sexual charm and get him out there without having to actually kidnap him."

"How would you kidnap him?"

"I'd have to buy a gun. There's no waiting period in Georgia, but there'd be a record of the sale."

"Gotcha."

"I really want to avoid that." Alice cleared her throat. "I said this in Vegas, but I'm not sure I've made this completely clear. Saving my children is my top priority above everything else. I'm going to do everything I can to get away with this, but if we start to run to the end of the hourglass, I'll do whatever it takes. If that means blowing his head off in broad daylight in front of a crowd of witnesses, so be it."

"Noted," said Nate.

"I promise you won't go down for this. If this all turns to shit, I'll tell them I forced you to help. I'll take the heat for everything."

"Thanks," said Nate. Though his area of expertise was more geared toward fajitas than criminal law, he was pretty sure that if he got busted trying to help her hide a dead body, Alice saying, "It was all me!" wouldn't necessarily be his Get-Out-Of-Jail-Free card. He also didn't trust that she *would* confess to the crime. She could say that the video—which she hadn't recorded yet—was made under duress. If he was just her pawn, why not let him share the blame? Or flat-out point her finger at him? Increase her chances of getting out of prison before her grandchildren went to prom.

That said, if the guy was a horndog, her plan really wasn't bad. If Alice could get him away from civilization without any witnesses, a man with a beautiful woman riding him probably wouldn't be thinking about how to protect himself if she pulled out a knife.

Despite his sarcastic outburst, Nate didn't really like the thought of her having sex with somebody else. Which was weird and almost deranged, since he didn't think of her as his real wife, or even his girlfriend. But prior to being gobsmacked, he'd cared about her a lot, and the idea of her having sex with another guy—especially when he was watching them in the car like some drooling pervert—didn't sit well with him.

He'd get over it, of course. He wouldn't let petty and irrational jealousy get in the way of the plan.

Though he did have another idea that would get in the way.

"What's his name?" Nate asked.

"I'm still not ready to tell you that."

"I can help watch for his routine. If you're doing the 'meet cute,' you don't want him to recognize you from somewhere else. I can follow him for a day."

"You've been beaten to shit. You can barely walk."

"I'll take a few aspirin."

"You're very memorable looking right now. You can't blend in. You're the one we'd need to worry about him seeing twice."

She was absolutely right. So Nate needed to try a new tactic.

"I can at least stalk him on social media."

"I've been doing that from the beginning."

Nate wondered if he could use her search history to find the name. Maybe? But most likely her computer was password protected, and she was clearing her search history or using private mode. She wouldn't plan a murder and then let the FBI pull up evidence of the crime on her browser. The information could probably be retrieved, but Nate wouldn't have any idea how to go about it.

Okay, he needed to switch tactics *again*.

"Here's the deal," he said. "I can't trust you."

"What are you talking about?" asked Alice. "You're the one who betrayed my trust!"

"I get that. But if I may be totally cold-hearted for a moment, this is *your* problem. Agreeing to help you is insane. If you're with-holding important information from me, that puts me even more at risk. I need to know who you're planning to kill, so I can do my own research."

"Obviously, I'm going to tell you who it is very soon. Just not yet."

"I need to know now. Starting this very second, we have to completely trust each other."

Alice stared at him, as if trying to find evidence of an ulterior motive in his expression. Nate tried to look sincere without trying too hard. Let his facial muscles fall into place naturally. Don't give anything away.

"Okay," she said. "His name is Shane Flagler."

"Thank you."

"He posts a lot of shitty TikTok videos."

"Good to know."

Nate had an idea. He didn't *want* to keep it from Alice, but it wasn't something they could discuss while they were being moni-tored. Though he wasn't sure there was anything he could do with this idea, it was at least worth investigating.

Yes, this was all to save kidnapped children, but they were still planning to murder an innocent man.

What if there was a way around that?

What if there was a way to fake it?

Shane Flagler didn't have to disappear forever. He had to disappear long enough for Alice to claim victory and get her kids back.

Nate had just received a brutal beating and a lecture about following the letter of the law, yet ignoring the spirit of it. But there was no rule against him speaking with the victim. In fact, since he was permitted to help Alice complete the task, it might be an appealing idea—something to help lure the guy to the spot where he would meet his doom. Nate hadn't come close to working out the logistics yet, but if he could speak with Shane Flagler and secretly send him a message, there might be a way to fool the asshole in the facemask into thinking that Alice had killed him.

Yes, he'd be betraying Alice's trust in a very similar manner to what he'd already done...but this was murder! She was going to slash some guy's throat while fucking him! Why not at least *try* to come up with a way to avoid that?

Unless the dude turned out to be a pedophile, he didn't deserve to die. He probably had loved ones who would be devastated. Maybe he had kids himself.

He wouldn't put Alice's children at risk. Wouldn't do anything to make Shane Flagler run to the cops.

Nate wasn't committed to this idea, but it was something to think about.

"I'm probably going to kill him tomorrow," said Alice.

"That soon?"

"Why wait? My deadline is coming up. I'd do it tonight, but you're in no condition to help."

Nate couldn't deny that. Right now he didn't feel like he could overpower an arthritic Dachshund. He expected to be in agony tomorrow, too, but he was confident he could push through if he needed to.

"You should go to bed," Alice said. "I'll sleep on the couch so I don't keep you up."

"You're staying over?"

"Yes. Is that okay?"

"Sure. But I can't stay here and plan. I have to go to work tomorrow."

"You're not going to work."

"Excuse me?" Nate asked.

"Look at you. They'd send you right home. You can't serve customers looking like that."

"I'm scheduled to work tomorrow, and we're short-staffed."

"Have you ever been to a restaurant where the server looks like he lost a bar fight? You'd turn people off their burritos."

"I don't look *that* bad."

"Would you like me to bring you a mirror?"

"Nah, I'll check."

Nate got up and made his way into the bathroom. He looked in the mirror, and...okay, yeah, he could see what she meant. He was a little grotesque. Obviously, paying customers wouldn't be able to see his chest, but his face was purple and yellow and swollen.

He couldn't pay their victim a secret visit if Alice was around, but he didn't know how to get rid of her.

Was there a way to send Alice a message?

Nate didn't know the size of this operation. But nobody had stopped him from visiting Renee. The man in the facemask seemed overworked and annoyed. Certainly there was a lot that Nate wasn't seeing, but this didn't *feel* like a large-scale outfit. He got his ass kicked in a parking garage.

He had no reason to doubt that Alice's necklace was real. And maybe they'd bugged her house. Maybe somebody had broken into his apartment while he was at work and placed hidden cameras and microphones. But were they monitoring his e-mails and text messages? Watching his every move? If they went into a crowded restaurant, would it really be impossible to convey a message to her?

Nate didn't think it would be. He was pretty sure they were relying on them not being willing to take the risk.

The problem was that Alice *wasn't* willing to take the risk, and if he did get a message across, she might lose her shit again.

But how could you fake a death if not everybody was in on the plan?

There was a lot to unravel here, but it would be really, really nice to get out of this mess with a clear conscience, and without jumping out of his skin every time he heard a knock at the door, thinking it was the FBI.

He didn't think faking the murder would be that hard. Do it in the dark. A few phony stabs to the chest. But, of course, both Alice and Shane would have to know what was going on.

As Nate looked at himself in the mirror, Alice stepped into the bathroom behind him. He flinched like a cheap horror movie jump scare. "It's okay," she said with an actual smile on her face. "It's just me."

Nate turned and smiled back. "Can't think of any reason I might be jumpy."

"It's a very strange set of circumstances, but I *am* still your wife. How about I take care of you and draw you a nice warm bath?"

"I don't have any of those fancy salts or bubble bath or anything like that."

"That's fine. Water and shampoo."

"I do know how to fill a bathtub with water."

"I know," said Alice. "But it's nice when somebody else does it. Go sit on the couch."

Nate did as he was told. Alice ran the water, and called him back in a few minutes later. She helped him out of his clothes, which was greatly appreciated, because he was in agony. She eased him into the tub, and he slid under the water to his neck. It felt incredible. He hadn't taken a bath since he was a kid. He'd really been missing out.

He could fall asleep right there. He wouldn't, though—drowning would not help get Alice's kids back.

Alice brought in a chair from the dining room and sat by the tub as he soaked. There was nothing romantic about it. Just one person taking care of another. It was very pleasant.

His mind kept coming back to the idea that somehow they could fake Shane's death.

It would be dark.

Alice could immediately turn around and pretend to dry heave. Nobody said she had to hold her necklace right up to the carnage. At least, he assumed nobody had.

If all three participants were clear on what needed to be done, how hard could it be?

He just needed a way to convey the plan to Alice.

And now he had an idea.

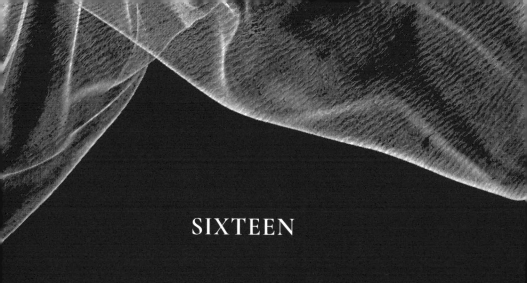

SIXTEEN

Nate had to play this carefully. Very, very carefully.

Think about what he was going to say. Phrase it so that the creeps listening in wouldn't suspect anything, but that his message still got across to Alice.

He let out a long, satisfied sigh. "This is really nice. Thank you."

"You're welcome."

"I know it was all a ruse, but we had some good times, right?" he asked. "There was a legitimate connection between us."

"There was, for sure."

Nate tried to think of exactly how their conversation in the Las Vegas hotel room had gone. He wanted to sound like he was simply rehashing a prior discussion, so she'd get a bit suspicious.

"If we met under different circumstances, do you think it would've worked out this way? I obviously don't mean us rushing into marriage; I just mean us being together."

"I think it would," said Alice. "I like you a lot, Nate."

"And the sex. The sex was good, right?"

"Yeah, it was."

"You weren't faking anything?"

"No."

"Are you sure?"

"Yes, I think I'd know if I'd been faking it or not."

"I mean, you'd tell me if you were, right?"

"When did you become so insecure?" Alice asked.

"I'm not insecure," said Nate. "Just curious. Honestly, I don't think there's anything wrong with a woman faking it."

Alice said nothing.

"Sorry if I'm babbling. I may have a concussion. I don't know, they say that women shouldn't fake it, but it avoids hurt feelings and awkwardness, and there are times when it's the right thing to do. Again, sorry if I'm babbling. What do you think?"

Alice reached over and placed her hand on his shoulder. She slid her fingers along it, which felt really good.

Then she jabbed her thumb into a large bruise, hard.

Nate let out a yelp of pain and sat upright, splashing water over the side of the tub.

"What the hell is wrong with you?" Alice demanded.

"Nothing! It was a simple question!"

"I know what you were trying to do!"

"I'm not allowed to talk about you faking orgasms?"

Alice picked up the eyeball charm on her necklace and held it to her mouth like a microphone. *"I will not be going along with this. It was him and him alone. I have completely, unequivocally, rejected the message he tried to send. I will finish the game without cheating. Please understand this."*

She slapped the same bruise.

"Goddamn it, Alice!" said Nate, trying to move away from her, although the bathtub didn't offer many options.

"I don't get it," she said. "I just don't get it. What the hell is wrong with you?"

"Nothing!"

"Are you a sociopath? Do you not care about what happens to my kids? Or are you purposely trying to get them killed because you hate me so much?"

"Of course not."

"Because you're sure behaving like you hate my guts and want to see me suffer. We just went through this, Nate!"

"I know we did," Nate admitted. He was floored by Alice's reaction. Even if she hadn't gone for the idea, he never would've imagined that she'd call him out like this. "But you're calling me a sociopath for trying to prevent you from having to murder somebody! I was trying to get us out of this without blood on our hands."

"You're toying with my kids' lives."

"No, I wanted to keep their mom out of prison, or from getting killed herself. The plan would've worked. If you hadn't had a meltdown and just absorbed the message I was sending, we could've figured this all out."

"Don't make plans," said Alice. "Don't think for yourself." She raised her hand as if to slap him again, but then seemed to think better of it. "You were supposed to help me, but now you've made things so much harder. I can't let you out of my sight. I'll have to babysit you the whole time."

"You don't have to babysit me."

"Yes, I do. If I leave you unattended, how do I know you won't run off and warn him that he's in danger?"

"I won't. I'll do whatever you say. You've broken my spirit. Congratulations."

"But I can't trust you. You lied to me."

"I'm pretty sure you don't get to criticize somebody for fibbing," said Nate.

"I confessed everything to you when I was allowed to do so, and I've been completely open since then. Meanwhile, you're sneaking around and trying to send secret messages about an idiotic plan."

"It wasn't idiotic. It would've worked."

"Whatever."

"I guess it's irrelevant. But I'm done. I'm not saying I'll do whatever you tell me to do, but I won't do anything without clearing it with you first. I promise."

"I wish I could believe you," said Alice.

"Not to be a douchebag, but you really don't have a choice. Don't want my help anymore? I'm happy to sit the rest of this out. I assume that's not what you want."

Alice gave him a look that quite honestly scared him. It was as if she was imagining jabbing her thumb into his bruise, sinking into the flesh as deep as she could. Then her expression softened.

"No," she admitted. "That's not what I want. Enjoy the rest of your bath." She walked over to the bathroom door, then turned back. "I'm going to keep your phone with me. I hope you don't have a problem with that."

Nate did, actually. But this probably wasn't the time to fight her on that. Especially since he'd have to leap out of the tub and sprint naked into the living room to retrieve it. In his current condition, she could almost certainly kick his ass and take it away from him.

He shrugged. "That's fine."

"I'm going to get some sleep. You should do the same when you're done. We've got a busy day tomorrow." Alice left the bathroom, shutting the door behind her.

The bath was no longer relaxing, so Nate pulled out the stopper, got out, and dried himself off. He wrapped a towel around his waist and left the bathroom. He half-expected to find Alice curled up in his bed as a power play, but no, she was lying on the couch, eyes closed. He could see a bulge in her front pocket that was either his cell phone or hers. He couldn't imagine that she was a sound enough sleeper for him to take it back without waking her up, and he really didn't need it for anything right now.

He was going to keep his promise.

Unless he found a good reason not to.

Nate woke up to a delicious smell. When he staggered out of his bedroom, there was a plate of scrambled eggs and toast waiting for him.

"Sorry the portion's so small," said Alice. "You only had one egg in the fridge. And no bacon." She sat at the table and poured some cold cereal into a bowl for herself.

"Thank you. You didn't have to do that."

"Trust me, I know."

Nate sat across from her and ate. The egg was perfectly seasoned. So if they stayed together, which they most assuredly would not, he'd have well-cooked and seasoned scrambled eggs on occasion. It was a dumb thought, but it was better than thinking about them planning a murder.

"How are you feeling?" Alice asked.

"Sore. I'll be fine."

"After breakfast, take some ibuprofen and a long, hot shower. Then we'll head out, and I'll show you where we're going to do it."

Nate stayed in the shower until Alice knocked on the bathroom door to ask if he was all right. It felt great and relaxed his muscles, but mostly he wanted to delay going out to view the future murder scene. He popped a few pain killers and got dressed, wearing blue jeans and a completely non-descript white T-shirt, so that he wouldn't stand out if the wrong person saw him.

When he emerged from the bathroom, Alice handed him his phone. "Call in sick," she said. "But don't say anything suspicious. I'll be listening."

Nate nodded and called his boss. He got Craig's voice mail and left a completely normal-sounding message saying he had a stomach bug and couldn't come in to work. He apologized profusely and promised to be in tomorrow.

"You may not be in tomorrow," said Alice after he hung up.

Nate shrugged. "I'll worry about that later."

She extended her hand for his phone.

"Seriously?"

"Yes."

Nate almost gave it to her, then shoved it into his pocket instead. "I'm not your hostage. You'll just have to trust me."

"If you're on it, and I can't see what you're doing, I'll have to assume the worst."

"I'll show you what I'm doing."

Nate didn't have any specific plan that involved his cell phone, but he didn't like the idea of her hanging onto it, especially if they were going into a dangerous situation. For all he knew, she'd be using his phone to compile evidence against him. And, yes, there was a petty power struggle involved.

They left his apartment building. "You drive," said Alice.

As soon as they got into his car, Nate's phone started ringing. He pulled it out of his pocket and glanced at the display. Josh. He held the phone up for Alice to see.

"What does he want?" she asked.

"I don't know. I haven't answered. I assume he's pissed because I called in sick."

"Pissed or worried?"

"I'm going to go with pissed. Mind if I answer?"

"Yeah, I do mind. Put it back in your pocket."

"It'll be weird if I don't answer."

"No, it won't. You're sick. You probably went back to bed. Put it in your pocket."

Nate did as he was told. He was frustrated and angry about it, but at this point, he needed to choose his battles. No need to bicker over every detail. To be fair, if the roles were reversed, he wouldn't want her having a conversation with a co-worker where she might send a secret message either.

He started the engine. "Where are we going?"

"Just drive," she said. "I'll direct you as we go."

NATE EXPECTED A MUCH LONGER DRIVE. INSTEAD, THEY STOPPED AT a small park. Secluded, yes, but not out in the middle of nowhere. From the park itself, you couldn't see any homes, but they weren't that far. Somebody screaming bloody murder would be heard.

"Is this really where you want to do it?" he asked, as they got out of the car.

Alice nodded. "The trees block everything. Nobody can see what's going on unless they just happen to be driving by, and there aren't any lights. We'd be doing it in almost complete darkness."

"I just thought we'd be out in the middle of nowhere. If he got away, he could be pounding on somebody's door begging for help in two minutes. And we can't bury the body here."

"I know. When I thought of the plan, I envisioned being deep in the woods. But I had to decide if it was more important to be far from civilization, or more important to keep him from figuring out what's going on. If we're looking for a private spot, this drive won't set off any red flags. If we go too far, he might wonder if I'm taking him someplace to murder him. So this isn't ideal, but if he feels completely comfortable, I can slash his throat quickly, and it won't matter if people live nearby."

"And if you don't slash his throat quickly, you're screwed."

"True," said Alice. "But you're a guy. If I offered you free sex, how far from the city could I lure you before you started to think something was fishy?"

"Not very far."

"See?"

"Maybe not even this far."

"That's a definite concern. I'll have to be persuasive."

"And if you're not?"

"Then we'll have to be flexible. You may get a text from me saying that the plan has completely changed."

"Oh, so I'm allowed to use my phone?" said Nate, much more sarcastically than he intended.

"I have to trust you. We can't not be in communication."

"I agree."

"I'll try to get him to park where your car is now," said Alice. "If not exactly there, at least close. Which means..." She walked over to some trees. "If you hide back here, you'll be completely out of sight but close enough to jump in and help if something goes wrong."

"And how exactly will I help?"

"You'll have a baseball bat. You can't kill him, and I would never ask you to even if you were allowed, but you can break his kneecap if necessary. You're just going to watch very carefully what is happening, and if you see things going wrong, you step in.

Hopefully that won't be needed, and you can just help me clean up."

"And then the fun begins. So do I just wait here for you to show up?"

"No," said Alice. "I was going to have you keep an eye on me as best you can. You don't have to be a master private investigator—keep your distance, but watch out for me. I'll text updates whenever I get a chance."

"Is that smart?"

"I wasn't planning to specifically reference the murder in my texts."

"Okay."

They got back in the car. Obviously, the murder wouldn't be happening in his vehicle, but he wondered how much blood sprayed from a slashed throat, and how difficult it would be to clean it out of the upholstery.

"How was that?" asked Alice.

"Good enough," said Nate, stopping the recording. "Thank you."

She'd left out most of the story, out of a quite understandable concern that making a video blaming Renee for her actions could be construed as a violation of the rules. She'd also refused to let Nate record it on his phone; instead, they bought a very inexpensive camera that didn't have an internet connection. But she had explained that he was an unwilling participant in the murder. It was better than nothing.

Nate opened his safe, put the camera inside, and locked it.

"Remember, only if the walls are closing in," said Alice.

"Right." And Nate meant it. He was pretty sure he could hold up to a bit of police interrogation. However, when he got a chance, he was going to move the camera to a new hiding spot. Alice didn't know the combination, but that didn't mean she couldn't steal the whole safe and fling it into a gravel pit.

They were going to do it. They were really going to kill this poor guy.

SEVENTEEN

"Whoopsie! Careful there!" said Shane Flagler as the curly-haired redhead almost spilled her iced coffee on him. She'd been looking at the floor as she walked and was on a collision course. Fortunately, he dodged in time and avoided having her splash her cold beverage all over his white shirt, which would've been the perfect way to close out this crappy day.

Working from home was great, but this customer service stuff was killing him. Dealing with angry, entitled people all day long was simply not the best way to retain his sanity. He wanted to quit, but this was his third place of employment in a year, and his resume was starting to look like it belonged to somebody who couldn't hold a job.

But at least he was off the clock now and could just relax.

"I'm so sorry," said the woman. "I should've been paying better attention."

"No problem at all." Shane gave her a friendly smile and continued waiting for his order.

"Staying up late?" the woman asked.

"Huh?"

"Coffee at nine o'clock."

"Oh, yeah. Caffeine doesn't really affect me. And I'm waiting for a panini."

"You come here for the food?"

"Sure," said Shane. "It's a perfectly good panini. Not the best in town, but it gets the job done."

"What kind of panini?"

"Ham and cheddar."

The woman nodded her approval. "That sounds good."

"It always is."

The woman took a sip of her coffee but didn't leave. "I've got a late night ahead of me."

"Do you?"

"My blind date was a no-show. So I'm going to stay up all night watching cartoons and eating ice cream."

"Sorry to hear that. Nothing wrong with cartoons and ice cream, though."

The woman still didn't leave. She seemed nervous and was making Shane a little uncomfortable. She scratched at her scalp—it kind of looked like she was wearing a wig.

"I'm Bethany," she said.

Shane hesitated. He wanted to give her a fake name, but any second now they'd call out his order. "I'm Shane."

"Do you go by Bob?"

"Nope."

"Then, hi, Shane. Nice to meet you." She extended her hand, and Shane shook it.

"Nice to meet you, Bethany."

"Sorry I almost spilled my coffee on you."

"It's totally okay." Was she hitting on him? She was certainly attractive, but there was something scary going on with her eyes, and after his last breakup, Shane was ready for his life to become a drama-free zone. He needed a lot of Zen right now.

"Order for Shane," said the employee, setting down a tray with his panini and coffee.

"Have a good night," Shane told Bethany, taking his tray to an empty table and sitting down. As he unwrapped the aluminum foil from his sandwich, she sat across from him.

"Mind if I join you?"

"Actually, I do," he said. "I'm sorry. I'm not trying to be rude. I don't know you, and I'm not looking to get involved with anybody right now."

"Not even looking for a friend?" she asked.

"I'm really not. Sorry."

"I'll leave you alone, I promise," she said. "I'm not interested in a relationship, I don't want any money, and I'm not going to cause any trouble. But if you want a friend, I'm here."

"I appreciate that. I'm good, though."

Bethany clenched her jaw. She nodded. "Okay. Enjoy your panini." She got up and left.

When he was eighteen, Shane would've been all over that. ("*You want to be friends? Tell me more!*") These days, nah. He almost thought she might have been trying to spill her coffee on him on purpose. Either this was some sort of con job, or she was horny and desperate. He wasn't interested in hooking up with somebody that desperate. Or anybody at all, right now.

He ate his panini, which, as always, was perfectly decent.

ALICE DIDN'T LOOK HAPPY AS SHE GOT INTO THE PASSENGER SEAT OF Nate's car. She slammed the door.

"I guess I don't need to ask how it went," said Nate.

"He didn't go for it at all. I was annoying him." She smacked her palm against the dashboard. "Shit."

Nate wanted to make a joke about her now having the fiery temper of a redhead, thanks to the wig, but decided that the joke probably wouldn't land right. "Well, we knew this could happen."

"I completely screwed it up. He dodged the coffee. The whole point was that he was going to have iced coffee all over him, and I'd insist on helping him get cleaned up. But the asshole's reflexes were too good."

"It's okay," said Nate. "This whole murder plan didn't hinge on the coffee. We'll just try again tomorrow."

"I thought I was going to see my kids tonight."

"I know. But we've got time."

Shane went to the same coffee shop almost every evening, around the same time, so they'd have another chance. Though he dreaded what was going to happen, Nate was also anxious for it to be over, and he wasn't looking forward to another day of anticipation.

"I have to go in to work tomorrow," he said.

"No."

"I'm going to get fired."

"You care more about your stupid waiter job than two innocent children?"

"Nope. Not at all. Me going into work doesn't put them in any extra danger. I assume you don't care if I get fired because you're laser-focused on your own problem...which, to be fair, is a pretty big problem. What you *should* care about is that if you're in any way tied to Shane Flagler's death, it won't look very good that your husband got fired for failing to show up to work."

"We've discussed this. I can't trust you."

"And I don't give a shit. I do give a shit about being unemployed and about the police wondering why I didn't come in to work the day Flagler went missing."

"That's a good point," Alice admitted. "We were planning to kill him tonight. Why didn't you think of that before you called in sick today?"

"Because I'm not a criminal mastermind."

"Don't you work until around nine-thirty?"

"Yeah, but you can text me if you need me to duck out early. He's not going to just jump in a car with you. You probably wouldn't be heading to the spot until after I'm off work anyway, and I'm not going to get fired if I have to leave a little early. But I can't have them cover a whole shift for me again."

"You're lying to me," said Alice.

Nate blinked in surprise. "Excuse me?"

"You just finished saying that you didn't want the cops to find out that you missed work on Shane's final night. Now it's okay to leave early."

"We're talking about leaving maybe half an hour early. It's not the same thing. I can just say I have a doctor's appointment or something. Look, you're asking me to be gone the entire day, which means they have to call somebody else in to work my shift, and I've already said that they're short-staffed. I just took off for our Vegas trip!"

"Will your excuse hold up if the police ask your boss why you left early on the night Shane Flagler was murdered?" asked Alice. "Considering that it's pretty fucking weird that your doctor's office would be open that late."

"Okay, I wouldn't actually say I had an appointment," said Nate. "I'd just say I was feeling sick again and needed to go home. Again, it's just half an hour. Maybe fifteen minutes. Honestly, if you talk to him at nine, you'll probably still be at the coffee shop by the time I clock out."

Nate felt like he was floundering, yet the irony was, he was telling her the truth. He had no intention of going behind her back. He just didn't want to lose his job.

"How stupid do you think I am?" asked Alice. "You talked to Renee, you tried to send me a secret message about faking the murder…why the hell would you think I'd let you out of my sight for eight hours?"

"For the reason I said. It will look bad if I called in sick the day of the murder."

"And it will look bad if you leave early."

"So I won't leave early. You can keep him talking for a bit. It's not like you were going to sprint out of the coffee shop to fuck him anyway. Flirt with him while I finish up my shift, and when I let you know I'm done, you can lure him to his death."

Without warning, Alice burst into tears.

"Why are you making everything about this so difficult?" she asked. "Why does everything have to be a fight? I just want Olympia and Peter back. Why can't you just fucking listen to me? *Why can't you just fucking listen to me?*"

There wasn't simply anguish in her voice. There was raw fury. Nate took a step back, as if Alice might grab him by the throat and squeeze until his eyeballs popped out of their sockets.

"I'm sorry," he said.

"If you're sorry, then quit doing it! Quit fighting me on every little thing! I hate this as much as you do, and I'm begging you to stop making it so hard!"

"I will. I'll call in sick. It's fine."

"I'll pay your bills while you're looking for a new job," said Alice. "I'll do whatever it takes."

"All right. We're good. It won't happen again."

Alice silently stared at him for a very long time. "Okay."

"So what do we do now? Nothing's going to happen until tomorrow night."

"I don't know."

"Should we watch a movie?"

"What movie?"

"I don't know," said Nate. "Something lighthearted."

"*Four Weddings and a Funeral?*"

"A funeral doesn't sound very lighthearted."

"It's really funny. You haven't seen it?"

"Nope."

"Hugh Grant. Andie MacDowell?"

"I know who's in it. I just haven't seen it."

"So, pizza and the movie?"

"Okay."

The movie was quite witty and delightful, but neither of them laughed even once.

"Nate?"

Shit. Nate had hoped to get Craig's voice mail.

"Uh, yeah, hi, Craig."

"Please tell me you're not calling in sick."

"I wish I wasn't," said Nate. "I really do. But I just can't get rid of this bug. I can't believe there's anything left in my stomach to vomit, but my body keeps finding a way. I'm just going to get as much rest as I can today."

"If you're that sick, you should go to the doctor."

"Yeah, that might be a good idea. If things get any worse, I'll go in. I think I'm mostly just going to sleep, though."

"What I mean is, you need to bring me a doctor's note."

"Okay, yeah, I guess I can do that."

"Let me be very clear," said Craig. "If you don't have a note from your doctor, don't bother coming in to work tomorrow."

"Oh."

"Sorry."

"No, no, that's fine. I totally understand. I'll go to the doctor."

"Thank you," said Craig. "Get better soon."

Nate disconnected the call and sighed.

"Does he want a doctor's note?" asked Alice.

"Yeah."

"I faked an X-ray. I can fake a note."

"Cool."

NATE SPENT THE DAY WORKING ON *FRANK, FRANK & FRANK*. OR, more accurately, he spent the day staring at the document on his laptop screen, without typing a single word.

This play sucked.

ALICE GOT IN THE CAR AND SLAMMED THE DOOR SO HARD NATE WAS surprised the windows didn't shatter. She pulled off her curly red-haired wig and tossed it into the back seat.

"It's okay if you're frustrated," he said, "but please don't break my car."

"He didn't show up."

"Well...that's disappointing, but we also knew that he doesn't go there every night. This happened to be one of the nights he didn't go. No big deal."

"It *is* a big deal. We're running out of time!"

"Right. But tonight isn't the last night. If he wasn't there today, he'll be there tomorrow."

"We don't know that."

"He's there almost every day," said Nate. "So, odds are, he'll be there tomorrow."

"Maybe I scared him away."

"Because you almost spilled coffee on him?"

"Because maybe he sensed something was up."

Nate shook his head. "You're overthinking it. He doesn't come to the coffee shop every day at 9:00 PM Eastern Standard Time like clockwork. He comes *most* days, around nine. Even if he thought something was a little off, there's no way you scared him away from his favorite coffee shop. It's the only one in the area that's open that late. Maybe he took a nap and didn't need it."

"Maybe we need to track him down."

"No!" said Nate. "We're not at the 'track him down' stage yet."

"Maybe we should be."

"You asked me to help you, so I'm going to help by vetoing that idea. The plan we have is the right way to do this. If we start to freak out, this could all go horribly wrong. If he's a no-show tomorrow, we might have to switch to Plan B, but we have to give it one more day."

"What if we're over-complicating it?" asked Alice. "Maybe I should just knock on his door and stab him when he answers."

"That's not a very good plan."

"I just want this to be over."

"So do I. But let's be patient. Stick to the plan."

That evening, they tried a double feature of gory horror movies, hoping that it would release some tension.

It didn't.

Nate left an early morning voice mail for Craig, apologizing for calling in sick yet again but assuring him his doctor had said it was the right thing to do. Craig called right back, but Nate didn't answer, and Alice confiscated his phone.

He didn't get shit done on his play.

They pulled into the parking lot of the coffee shop around 8:45. Alice, who Nate had to admit looked damn good as Bethany the Redhead, went inside.

Nate's face was looking quite a bit better, but still showed ample evidence of his beating, so his job was to stay in the car unless absolutely necessary.

At 9:04, he watched Shane Flagler walk inside the building.

EIGHTEEN

As Shane waited for his order, he noticed the redhead from the last time he was here. She sat at a table, looking at her cell phone, nibbling a muffin.

He kept sneaking glances at her as he stood by the counter. As far as he could tell, she hadn't noticed he was there. Her eyes never left her phone.

"Order for Shane."

She looked up as Shane picked up his coffee. He nodded and gave her a polite smile. She smiled back.

The woman—Beth? Bethany?—did have a very nice smile. And this time she was wearing a very tight red dress that showed off significantly more cleavage than the last time he saw her.

She waved.

He walked over.

"Hi," he said. "Remember me?"

"The man I almost drenched with coffee? Of course." She

He sat down next to her. Wow. Her dress was *short.* "Bethany, right?"

She nodded. "And you're...shoot, I'm sorry..."

"Shane."

"Shane! Yes! I knew it started with an S. How've you been, Shane?"

"Not too bad. Work sucks. But what else is new, right?"

Bethany laughed. "Right."

"How are you?"

"Good, good. My work also sucks."

"What do you do?"

"Spreadsheets. Lots and lots of spreadsheets."

"Do you come here a lot?" Shane asked. Then he gave her a sheepish smile. "Wow, look at me, asking the 'Do you come here often?' question. That's not an opening line. I'm here all the time, so I wasn't sure if you were too and we just don't see each other, or what."

"I'm new in town," said Bethany. "This is only my third time here. I really liked their coffee, so I kept coming back. I know that's silly, since Atlanta probably has hundreds of coffee shops, and I should try more of them, but I'm not always very adventurous. In some areas. In other areas, I'm *very* adventurous."

"What brings you to Atlanta?"

"Family. My mom is sick."

"Oh, I'm sorry to hear that."

"Me too."

"Am I being too nosy if I ask what's wrong with her?"

"Not at all, but I want to stick to fun topics. What do you like to do that's fun, Shane?"

Shane shrugged. "I don't know. I like to paint."

"Are you good at it?"

"No, I'm very bad."

"Tell me something you're good at."

"I don't know."

"You're good at *something*. Think hard."

"My fantasy draft football picks did pretty well last year."

"Okay, yes, I guess that counts. What else are you good at? What else do you enjoy?"

"Cooking, maybe?" said Shane. "I wouldn't necessarily say I'm *good* at it. I'd never open my own restaurant. I'm not a gourmet chef or anything. I'm okay. Maybe I'm okay because I'm the only one who eats it. I don't use a lot of seasoning or anything like that. But if I'm not too busy I enjoy it. Not my favorite thing to do in the world."

"What *is* your favorite thing to do in the world? What gives you the most pleasure?"

"Hmmm. I'm not sure. Fishing? I haven't gone fishing in a while, maybe a few years, but...fishing?"

"Fishing," said Bethany.

"Yeah."

Bethany scratched her scalp. There it was. The nervous, twitchy thing that had made him a little edgy before. The conversation was playful, but Shane got the impression it wouldn't be difficult to make her scream in frustration or burst into tears. There was something wrong beneath the surface.

"Maybe I could go fishing with you someday," she said.

"That would be fun. What kind of fishing do you enjoy?"

"I don't know what kinds of fishing there are. I would go with whatever you wanted to do."

"There's fly fishing, there's lure fishing, and so on. There's river fishing, there's lake fishing, there's deep sea fishing..."

"Let's do deep sea fishing. We'll catch us a shark."

"I've never actually gone shark fishing. Mostly I do fly fishing in a river. Try to catch bass. We could try it, though."

"I was kidding," said Bethany. She scratched her scalp again. "I wasn't really suggesting we try to catch a shark."

"Well, people do. Shark fishing is a real thing."

"Do you want to get out of here?"

"And go where?" Shane asked.

"Somewhere private."

"Oh. Oh, okay. You mean…"

"Yes."

Shane grinned. "That's very kind of you. What I'd like to do is take you out on a proper date. An actual restaurant—I won't make you endure my mediocre cooking."

"When?"

"Saturday?"

"Today's Tuesday."

"Right."

Bethany's smile did not reach her eyes. "I can do Saturday. But what could we do before that?"

"I don't know. I mean, Saturday's fine, right? There's no need to rush into anything, unless you have a terminal illness." Shane suddenly felt a bit of mental panic. "I apologize if you have a terminal illness. That was insensitive."

Bethany hesitated just long enough to make it uncomfortable. "It's fine. Here's my story. I'm a cancer survivor, and getting through it was a very long, awful process, but I came out on the other side. It left me with the mindset that I should go for what I want. Live in the moment. No regrets. When I look at you, I see something I want, and I think we could have a fantastic adventure tonight, and then go our separate ways. Or not. Up to you."

Shane let out a nervous chuckle. "That's very forward."

"Like I said, I go for what I want."

"I respect that. I admire it."

Shane was no stranger to one-night stands. It had been a while, sure, but he didn't have a policy of, "No, milady, we must not join bodies until we know our love is true!" But while Bethany was attractive and friendly, there was something…*unsafe* about her. Not from a sexually transmitted diseases standpoint (though after an unpleasant adventure with pubic lice, Shane was much more wary) but simply because she did not seem to be one hundred percent stable.

"I'm glad you admire it," she said.

"I do. That said, I'm *not* impulsive, but I would love to take you out to a very nice Italian restaurant Saturday night."

"Unlimited breadsticks?"

"Much nicer than that. The lasagna tastes like an Italian grand-mother made it."

"All right, yeah. It's a date."

"Awesome."

"You do understand that when I said 'fantastic adventure' I was talking about sex, right?"

"I did think that was where you were going with it, yes."

"And you're turning me down?"

"No. If everything goes well, I'm giving us more time to antici-pate it. Not that I'd have any expectations of you, obviously. It's not why I offered to take you out. Enthusiastic consent."

Bethany looked down at the table. A tear trickled down her cheek. "It's because I'm ugly, isn't it?"

"What? No. Of course not."

"It's all right. I understand."

"That's not it at all. You're beautiful. Look, I'm a gentleman, okay? I don't…go off on adventures with women I've just met."

"Maybe you should start. You might like it."

"Look, Bethany, I'm going to be completely honest with you. I'm not really digging the vibe here. You seem very sweet, and you're the furthest thing from ugly, but I'm not feeling a connection, and I think I'm just going to head off." He pushed back his chair.

"Did I say something wrong?"

"No, no, you're fine. I'm just not feeling it." He stood up. "Welcome to Atlanta, though. I'm sure you'll make a lot of good friends."

"Wait, hold on, don't go yet," said Bethany. "Shit, that's probably my mom. Give me just a second." She took out her cell phone and tapped out a text message, then she shoved it back into her pocket. "She still treats me like I'm in high school. Anyway, I'm sorry if I came on too strong. I was trying to be a fantasy come true. I was too aggressive, and I should have done a better job reading the room. It was my fault. I'll scale it back, I promise."

"I'm sorry, but no. I'm not interested."

"Really?"

"Really. You won't be lonely. It's a big city."

"Could you at least give me a ride home?"

"No."

"It's not far."

"No." Shane picked up his coffee and left.

Nate cursed as he got the text message from Alice: *Going badly.*

He wondered if Alice had messed it up, or if Shane was simply too difficult to seduce. Maybe a combination of both. It didn't matter.

This meant he had to get involved, which sucked. He didn't want to be part of the aftermath, much less the setup.

He got out of his car and walked toward the entrance. There were a few cars in the parking lot but no other people. Hopefully it stayed that way. His job now was to wait for Shane and Alice to come out and play his role convincingly.

He tried to make himself feel intimidating. His recent ass-kicking worked as part of the performance; hopefully his bruises would give the impression he wasn't afraid of a good fight.

Shane walked out of the coffee shop. Alice followed a moment later.

"Hey!" Nate shouted.

Shane looked over, thinking he was talking to him.

"Bethany!" Nate shouted, angrily. He strode forward toward them.

The key to this plan, which was the emergency backup, was that Shane would not simply go on his merry way, choosing not to get involved. But they hadn't been in the coffee shop very long, and it was entirely possible that Shane would, indeed, just walk to his car.

But he didn't. He stopped, and Alice stopped beside him.

"What are you doing here?" she asked.

"Looking for you."

"You're not supposed to be this close to me."

Nate took a step back. "Better?" They hadn't rehearsed exactly what they were going to say because they didn't want it to sound scripted. Nate was kind of pleased with, "Better?"

"You need to leave," said Alice.

"I'm going to get a coffee," said Nate. "Is that okay? Is getting a coffee okay? I mean, you're holding a coffee. Am I not entitled to a coffee, too? Is it okay, Princess Bethany, if I go inside and get myself a coffee?"

Was he overplaying it? Nate was starting to think he was overplaying it. He was paying close attention to Shane. For this to work, they needed to end it at the sweet spot where Shane was concerned about the domestic dispute playing out in front of him, but not fearful for his own safety.

Alice took a step closer to Shane. Nate was pleased to see Shane take a very small step closer to her, as if some protective instinct took over.

"That's fine," said Alice, in a whisper. "Get a coffee."

Nate glanced at Shane and *almost* said, "Who the fuck is this? Your boyfriend?" But, no. That could backfire. One, it could make Shane decide that he wanted absolutely no part of this, or two, it could make Shane decide that he needed to take care of this problem right now. Nate did not want Shane to beat the shit out of him right here in this parking lot.

Alice gave Nate a very tiny nod. He'd done his job. He walked past her and went into the coffee shop.

"THANK YOU," SAID BETHANY.

"Who was that?" Shane asked.

"My ex. I have a restraining order against him, but he's got a rich daddy, and he feels invulnerable."

"Does he live in Atlanta?" Shane wasn't necessarily trying to poke holes in her story, but if she was new to the city, that was a pretty fast timeframe to have a relationship, break up, and then file for and receive a restraining order.

Bethany shook her head. "No. He doesn't mind long drives. That's what's scary."

"You should call the police."

"Oh, I will. But right now I just want to get the hell out of here." Bethany wiped a tear out of the corner of her eye and took out her cell phone. She seemed genuinely shaken by the encounter, although from the way the guy looked, Shane was pretty sure Bethany could kick his ass if it came to that.

"I'll walk you to your car," said Shane.

"I don't have one. I'll wait for an Uber."

"No, it's okay. I'll give you a ride out of here."

"Are you sure?" asked Bethany. "That would be really, really nice of you. I won't be weird, I promise."

"It's totally fine. Let's go."

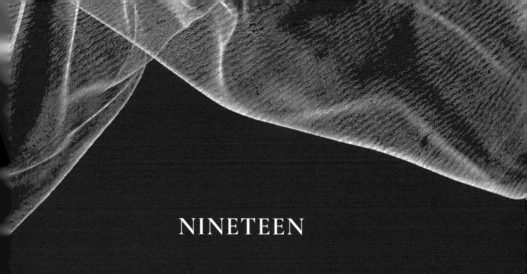

NINETEEN

N ate watched Alice get into the car with Shane. Perfect.
Obviously, the perfection of this moment was marred by the fact that Alice was going to murder the guy who was kind enough to drive her away from her abusive ex. For now, Nate just needed to focus on the plan. There'd be plenty of time for self-loathing later.

Nate watched through the coffee shop window as they drove out of the parking lot.

He waited a couple of minutes, just in case, then hurried to his car.

"THANKS AGAIN," SAID BETHANY. HER LEATHER PURSE WAS ON HER lap, and she nervously played with the strap. "This really means a lot to me."

"No problem at all," said Shane. "Look, I'm sorry I refused you a ride earlier."

"No, no, that was my fault. I was off my game. And by that, I mean I have no game. I don't come on to strange guys in coffee shops, or bars, or fuckin' Laundromats, or wherever. That's not me. I was just thinking, new city, fresh start, I should go after what I want. I apologize for messing it all up."

"I promise you it's fine. Don't give it another thought."

Bethany wiped her eyes. "Then I won't. I'll just do my best to be charming company."

"Where am I dropping you off?"

"Oh, anywhere. I can get an Uber."

"I can take you home."

"Are you sure? It's probably twenty minutes away."

"In Atlanta traffic? That's nothing. That's a trip around the corner."

Bethany laughed. "Maybe half an hour, then."

"Where do you live?"

"East Point."

"That's close to where I'm headed anyway," said Shane.

It wasn't. They'd already driven past his apartment, and he had absolutely no reason to go toward East Point. But now that he actually had Bethany in his car, he had to admit the possibilities of an attractive woman coming on to him like this were intriguing. He'd be careful in case this was some kind of con job, but maybe he'd see where things led.

"Convenient," said Bethany. "I like making things easy."

"Are you a natural redhead?" Shane asked. She obviously wasn't —Shane just wanted to see if she'd lie to him.

"Nah." She tapped her hairline. "Totally a wig. New city, new hair."

"What's your natural color?"

"What do you hope it is?"

"Blonde?"

"You're in luck."

"Nice."

"Maybe I'll prove it to you," she said. She seemed to take a moment to let that sink in. "By taking off my wig, of course."

"Of course."

"I'd say that the carpet matches the drapes, but there is no carpet, if you know what I mean."

Shane chuckled.

Bethany put her hand over her mouth to stifle a laugh. "Oh my God, I can't believe I said that. I promised to behave, and I'm being filthy. I am so sorry. I don't know what's gotten into me today."

"It's fine."

"I swear, I'm not some depraved horndog."

"I believe you."

"I'm not sure you do."

"I'm willing to believe that you're not depraved," said Shane. "The other part will take some convincing."

"How do I convince you of that?" asked Bethany. "It's hard to prove a negative."

"True."

"I guess I could prove it by *not* putting my hand on your leg."

"That would be a start."

Bethany placed her hand on his leg.

"Well, shit," she said.

NATE'S ANXIETY LEVEL, ALREADY HIGH, SPIKED WHEN HE SAW THE red and blue flashing lights in his rearview mirror.

It was fine. It was fine. He hadn't done anything wrong yet.

He pulled over to the side of the street, hoping the cop had somebody else in mind, but no, he was the lawbreaker. He rolled down his window, took his driver's license and proof of insurance out of his wallet, got his registration out of the glove compartment, and waited.

The cop walked toward Nate's vehicle. He looked like somebody who would say, *"Looks like you have a broken taillight,"* and then shatter it with his foot. But to be fair, Nate was making that observation based on very little information, and he was probably just freaking out.

"Hi," said Nate, handing over the documents before the cop asked for them.

"Thank you," said the cop. "Do you know why I pulled you over?"

"Uh, no."

"Did you see that stop sign two blocks back?"

"Yeah. I stopped."

The cop shook his head. "A rolling stop is not a stop, sir."

"Oh. I thought I'd stopped all the way."

"Nope. And it's going to cost you $200."

"Okay. That's fair."

"I'm going to run your plate, and I'll be right back."

"Thank you."

The cop returned to his vehicle. Nate wanted to slap himself in the face, but did not. Rolling stop. What kind of dumbass accessory to murder would do a rolling stop when he was trying to avoid drawing any attention to himself? Now he couldn't simply tell the prosecuting attorney he'd been in his apartment all evening. How could he have been so careless? What an absolute idiot moron dipshit.

He should just tell Alice that he had to bail.

But she was already in Shane's car.

That wasn't his problem. Let her do it herself.

He sighed.

No. He'd help her save her children.

He sent her a text.

"Sorry," said Bethany. "My mom again."

"No problem. Do what you've gotta do."

"She was like this even before she got sick. You'd think I was fifteen." She tapped away at the screen of her phone. "So, I have a question for you."

"Sure."

"Should I tell my mom I'll be home late?"

"Oh, uh, no, don't do that," said Shane. "You should go home if she needs you. You moved here to take care of her, right?"

"Yes, but she doesn't need me to be there every minute."

"No, no, I don't want to cause any issues. There's no rush for anything to happen. I'd still love to take you to that Italian place on Saturday, and we can go from there."

"She wasn't asking me to come home. She was just asking how I'm doing. She does that every ten minutes."

"Still…"

"I don't have to go home. I promise."

"Okay. I'm just trying not to get involved in any family drama."

"Here, I'll make you feel better."

ALICE'S PICTURE POPPED UP ON NATE'S CELL PHONE AS A CALL FROM her came through. What the hell? Had she been forced to abandon the plan? Had she killed Shane already?

He hadn't actually told her he'd been pulled over, just that he'd been delayed by about fifteen minutes. He didn't want to freak her out more than he, himself, was currently freaked out.

Were you allowed to take a phone call while you were waiting for a cop to make sure there wasn't a warrant out for your arrest? Nate supposed that as long as he wasn't chatting away when the cop came back, it would be okay.

"Bethany?" he answered, deciding that was smarter than "Alice."

"Hey, Dad," she said. "I just wanted to make sure everything was okay with Mom. I'm sure it is, but I wanted to check in case I don't come back right away."

Should Nate try to lower his voice to sound more like a fifty-year-old? He didn't want to sound ridiculous. Instead, he faked a cough. "Oh, yeah, your mother's fine. You know how she is."

Shit! Nate saw in the rearview mirror that the cop was coming back.

"Yeah, I know," said Alice. "I know very, very well."

"I've got everything under control, so don't you worry. I'll see you later." Nate hung up the phone, hoping he'd done what he needed to do.

The cop walked up to the window. He handed Nate his documentation and a $250 ticket. Nate decided not to ask why the ticket was fifty dollars more than he'd been told.

"Remember, a rolling stop is not a stop. The signs aren't just there to look pretty. Now what are you going to do the next time you see a stop sign?"

"I'm going to come to a complete stop."

"Very good. You have a pleasant evening, sir."

"I will."

"It's all good," said Bethany. "Mom's fine."

"You didn't have to do that," said Shane. "I believed you."

"I get it; you don't want to interfere in any family drama."

"Well, I didn't think there was drama. I just wanted to make sure your mom would be okay. I didn't realize your dad was there to take care of her."

"Dad has his own issues, but I'm not there to be their live-in nurse. Just trying to keep an eye on things. And it helps me out while I'm trying to find a job and a place of my own." Bethany put her cell phone back into her pocket.

One thing Shane noticed, and it was probably no big deal, was that she'd kept her cell phone slightly tilted away from him. It didn't make him intensely suspicious—it could easily be an unconscious habit to keep her phone away from prying eyes. He didn't think he could get away with asking her to show him the text message exchange between her and her mom. He'd just have to be very aware of where his wallet was at all times, not drink anything she offered him, and not give her any personal information.

"Anyway," she continued, "I don't have a curfew, so what would you like to do about that?"

"What would you like to do?"

"You already know what I'd like to do."

"Do I?"

Bethany nodded. "But first, how about you pull into that convenience store? I'll go get us a couple of drinks."

"I don't need a drink. I've got my coffee."

"How about a popsicle?"

"A popsicle?"

"Sure. You like popsicles, right?"

"Yeah. I haven't had one since I was eleven or twelve."

"What flavor do you want?"

"What flavors do they have?"

"I have no idea."

"Surprise me," said Shane.

He pulled up in front of the convenience store, turned off the car engine, and removed his seatbelt.

"No, no, you stay put, I've got it," said Bethany. "My treat."

She got out of the car and went inside.

For a moment, Shane wondered if he should drive away.

Nah. He'd stick it out. It might be very much worth it.

NATE DROVE TOWARD THEIR MEETING PLACE, DOING A COMPLETE stop at every stop sign.

Fuckin' Nate.

It should've been very easy to get to the Murder Spot before them. He didn't have to floor the gas pedal and take shortcuts through people's yards; he just had to drive straight there, while Bethany killed a few minutes by accidentally giving Shane incorrect directions.

But he was going to be about fifteen minutes late. And since Shane was already suspicious of her, she couldn't steer him too far from their destination, in case he decided it was all too much and kicked her out of the car before they got there.

So now she had to kill time in a convenience store.

Which would probably put her on a security camera. But nothing was going to actually happen in the store, and Shane wasn't with her, and she was wearing this itchy wig, and presumably there was nothing unusual about somebody buying a couple of popsicles, so it would be all right.

She felt oddly calm about the upcoming murder. She just wished Shane would quit being such a pain in the ass.

"THEY DIDN'T HAVE INDIVIDUAL ONES," SAID BETHANY, GETTING back in the car. "Just pick a flavor and we'll throw away the rest of the box."

Shane tore open the box, which was properly sealed. There was enough illumination that he could see the flavors, but it was dark enough that he could pretend otherwise. He turned on the overhead light, took out a grape one, and discreetly checked for tears in the wrapper. It looked fine. How could she poison a frozen treat, anyway? She couldn't just inject it with a hypodermic needle.

"What flavor do you want?" he asked. "Or do you want me to surprise you?"

"Surprise me."

He took out an orange one and gave it to her. She tore open the wrapper and slid the popsicle into her mouth. Okay, if she was willing to have a random one, he could safely assume the popsicles were untainted. He tore open his grape one, then started the engine.

"Let's just enjoy them here," said Bethany.

"Sure thing." Shane turned the car off.

Bethany slid the popsicle back and forth between her lips, then burst out laughing. "I'm sorry. I can't pretend it's a penis. I'll have to find some other way to be alluring."

Shane laughed as well. "Then I, too, will not pretend my popsicle is a dick."

"A good choice for both of us."

Shane bit off the end of his. "Not a lot of grape flavor in this."

"No?"

"There's a teeny tiny little hint of grape. Other than that, I'm tasting...tap water."

"The orange one is fine. Wanna taste?"

She held the popsicle out to him. Shane licked the edge.

"Oh, yeah, orange is way better."

"We have plenty more. Or we could share this one."

"Let's share."

Plenty of vehicles were parked on the street, so there was no reason to think there'd be a problem if Nate left his car behind. From there, it would be a three-minute walk to the park. He took the aluminum baseball bat out of his back seat, closed the door, locked the car, and immediately had a dizzy spell so intense he fell to his knees.

He tried to breathe deeply and wait it out, desperately hoping that a well-meaning neighbor wouldn't come out and ask if he needed help.

His vision was completely blurry, and he felt like he was going to throw up.

He'd be fine. He'd be okay.

Was that the sound of a door opening?

Crap. Would a neighbor assume he needed medical attention, or that the bruised-up dude with the baseball bat was up to no good?

He forced himself to stand up, then braced himself against his car.

Waited for his vision to clear.

He couldn't tell how long he stood there. At least a couple of minutes. But when he could see again, nobody was there.

He waited a couple more minutes, until he was confident he could walk without falling on his face, and then headed toward the park.

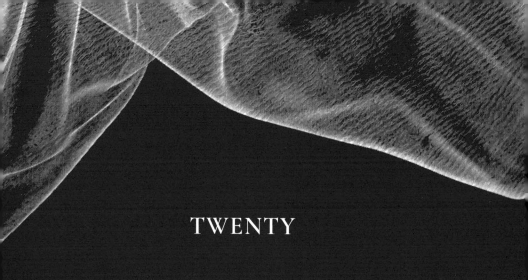

TWENTY

S hane watched as Bethany threw the box of popsicles away. He should have said, "No, no, let me throw them away," but he didn't like the idea of her being alone in his car, even if it was just long enough for him to walk to the garbage container and back. He was mostly convinced she really was just trying to get laid, but he also wasn't quite ready to let his guard down.

She got back in the car and stuck out her tongue. "Is it orange?"

"A little."

"Good thing I didn't have blue raspberry."

"It wouldn't have bothered me."

"Yeah?" asked Bethany. "Not afraid of a blue tongue on you?"

"Nope."

"Good to know for next time. You ready?"

"Definitely." Shane turned on the engine. "All right, I want to make sure I'm totally clear on this. No misread signals. The plan is for us to sleep together, right?"

"You are absolutely right. Well, there won't be any sleep

involved, but, yes, what you think is going to happen is exactly what is going to happen. If you're up for it, of course."

"I am."

"Then let's go."

"I'd ask 'your place or mine?' but you're staying with your parents, and I have a roommate." This was not true. He didn't want Bethany to know where he lived. "Is Holiday Inn okay?"

"Oh, we don't need a hotel," said Bethany. "I've got a place we can go."

"Where?"

"It's a park. Nice and secluded."

"We don't have to go to a park," said Shane. "I'll cover the cost of the hotel, no problem."

"There's no reason for that."

"I don't want to worry about somebody driving by, or walking up to the car, or the cops busting us for indecent exposure. I want to relax. Have fun like adults, not horny teenagers sneaking out of the house."

"I have fond memories of being a horny teenager sneaking out of the house," said Bethany.

"Me too. I also had sex with my girlfriend in her dorm room while her roommate tried to study for finals. That doesn't mean I want to do it now."

"How about we compromise? Start at my spot and then move to the hotel?"

"Or we could start at the hotel, and I could treat you like a princess. Let's get a room with a Jacuzzi. Room service. Champagne. We'll do it up right. I don't want you to think of me as some dude who fucked you in a park—excuse me for being crude."

Bethany put her hand on his leg again, inches from his crotch. "I appreciate your efforts at wooing me," she said. "I promise you, they're not necessary. I want it down and dirty, in your car, in a park, where The Hook might be lurking."

"The Hook?"

"You don't know the story of The Hook?"

"Captain Hook?"

"Campfire story. Serial killer with a hook for a hand. A couple is making out in their car, and when they drive away, they find a hook dangling from the car handle."

"So they basically ripped his hand off?"

"Yeah."

"Maybe I had heard that one. It's been a while."

"I'm not saying I want to re-enact the story of The Hook. I'm saying that I want you to drive me to that park and let me suck your cock."

Shane started to speak, but his mouth had gone dry. He wished he still had his popsicle. "That's not really me," he finally said. "I'm sorry."

"You're turning me down?"

"I'm just saying that a hotel would be more fun. We wouldn't have to worry about getting caught. We'd have more room to maneuver. I could make you feel incredible."

"Okay, Shane, I'm going to give you a very useful piece of life advice. When a woman offers to go down on you, you let her choose the place. What you're saying feels sleazy. If you want to take me to a fancy place with silk sheets, okay, but I'm not somebody you bang at a cheap motel."

"Well, it's a hotel, not a motel. And it's not that cheap. You can't rent a room at the Holiday Inn by the hour."

Bethany opened the door. "Goodbye, Shane. I hope you get to go fishing again soon."

"Wait," said Shane. "We can discuss this."

"I'm listening."

"I'll go with your compromise. We'll go to the park for a bit, but then you have to let me take you to a hotel. I promise it'll be nice. If you don't like the room, we'll find another one. It doesn't have to be the Holiday Inn, it can be...I don't know what the nicer hotels are around here, but we'll find one."

Bethany closed the door again. "That's fair."

<small>ON OUR WAY.</small>

Nate read the text and prayed that he wouldn't get hit with another dizzy spell. He was feeling queasy, but his vision was clear, so hopefully he'd be okay.

He was well-hidden in the bushes—he could even stand up—but he was paranoid as hell, as if any moment he might feel a tap on his shoulder and have somebody say, *"Who the fuck are you spying on, pervert?"* The bat had already slipped out of his hand once because he was perspiring so much.

But he might not have to do anything. Just watch. Help her clean things up afterward...which would be absolutely horrible, but wouldn't require him to actually participate in the murder of an innocent human being.

He'd hope for the best.

Well, no, the best would be for Renee to say, *"You know what? After some reflection and personal growth, I've decided that you're right. This game is silly. Here are Olympia and Peter, safe and sound."* That outcome was, he suspected, quite unlikely.

He continued to wait, hoping he wouldn't have a nervous breakdown before they arrived.

"TURN RIGHT," SAID BETHANY. "THERE IT IS. SEE, THAT'S NOT SO bad, is it?"

"Kind of dark," said Shane, as he drove into the park.

"That's why we're here. We don't want a big spotlight shining on us."

Shane parked and shut off the engine. They were in a reasonably nice area, and the park didn't look like the kind of place where drug deals would take place or you'd step on needles. There was a plastic slide, a swing set with two swings, and not much else.

"This looks okay, I guess," he said.

"Admit it, it's kind of fun, right? A little spooky?"

Shane was not a big fan of incorporating spookiness into his sex life, but he was willing to play along for now. The interior light went out, leaving them in almost complete darkness.

"Are you sure nobody's around?" he asked.

"Yes. The Hook is long gone."

"For real, are you sure nobody's around?"

"I haven't done a sweep of the perimeter, no. You've been with me the whole time. Does it look like anybody's around?"

"I don't know. I can't see."

"If you'd like me to turn on the flashlight on my phone and look around for Peeping Toms, I'm happy to. But unless they're flying a night-vision drone at the right angle to see into your car, they aren't going to get much of a show." She slid her fingers over his crotch. "Nobody can see what I'm doing. It's totally safe."

"You're right, you're right," said Shane.

"I'm not a mind-reader, but it feels like you're already getting into the mood."

"Yeah."

"Take your pants off."

Shane unzipped his pants, lifted up, and tugged them down.

"No, I mean all the way. Shoes off. I want you to have full range of leg motion when I climb on you."

"Oh, yeah, sure." Shane bent down to try to untie his shoes, though it was difficult with the steering wheel in the way. "There are a couple of condoms in the glove compartment."

"And I've got some in my purse. We're well-prepared."

Shane tried to keep the fumbling to a minimum. He managed to get his shoes off without too much embarrassment and then removed his jeans.

"Underwear too."

Shane pulled off his briefs.

"Wow," said Bethany. "You are *ready*. Damn."

She leaned over, putting her face in his lap.

NATE'S EYES HAD ADJUSTED TO THE DARK, AND THOUGH HE couldn't see perfectly what was happening, he got the basic gist. When Alice disappeared from sight, he knew exactly what was happening inside the car, and it bothered him.

Which was fucking stupid.

He had *much* more important things to worry about. Any minute now, he'd be longing for a return to the days when she was just giving the guy a blowjob. There was going to be a gout of arterial blood making a grisly pattern on the glass, and his weird-ass childish jealousy would be a thing of the past.

He really hoped he didn't have to use the baseball bat.

AT THIS POINT, SHANE WAS SUFFICIENTLY CONVINCED THAT Bethany was indeed a cancer survivor whose new approach to life was "Go after what you want."

"Oh, Christ, that's good," he said, running his fingers through the curly hair of her wig. "Oh my God. Yeah, keep doing that. Just like that."

This was paradise. Why had he ever doubted her? Hell, even if it *was* a con, it was worth it. She knew exactly what she was doing, and she seemed to love doing it.

After about a minute, she pulled her mouth away.

"Your turn?" Shane asked.

She shook her head. "I wanna ride you."

"Yeah, yeah, ride me. That's a good idea. Let's do that."

"Let's trade places. Sit in the passenger seat."

"Right, right." Shane opened the door. "Good idea. Great idea."

SHANE, WEARING NOTHING BUT SOCKS AND A SHIRT, GOT OUT OF THE car. He was extremely hard and extremely well-endowed. Nate wanted to look away, but the unwelcome sight of another man's dick should not distract him from his role in this nightmare.

Alice got out of the car on her side. She removed her panties, then smoothed down her dress. She glanced over in his direction, but he assumed she couldn't see him in the dark through the bushes.

Her victim, still rock-hard, walked around the front of the car over to the passenger side. They gave each other a quick kiss on the lips, and then Shane got inside the car. Alice climbed in on top of him, then pulled the door shut.

Nate felt physically ill.

Now, though, it was because he knew what was about to happen.

What he should *stop* from happening…?

Yes, the lives of kidnapped children were at stake, but Alice was about to slash some guy's throat! And he was going to let it happen! He'd *helped* it happen! Fuck!

BETHANY SAT ON SHANE'S LAP, FACING HIM, NOT ACTUALLY LETTING him inside her yet. She opened her purse and took out a condom. She tugged at the wrapper a couple of times. "Damn it."

"Here, I've got it." Shane tore the wrapper open with his teeth, removed the condom, and tossed the wrapper onto the floor. He unrolled it over his penis.

"I'm surprised it fits," said Bethany. "I bet you have extra-large ones in the glove compartment."

Shane smiled and said nothing.

She lifted up, adjusted her position, and very slowly began to slide down him. The condom was lubricated, but there was still some resistance.

"You okay?" he asked.

Bethany nodded. "You're bigger than I'm used to. That's all. Take it as a compliment."

With some effort, she slid all the way down. She gave him a passionate kiss and began to slide up and down his shaft.

Shane put his hands on her breasts, resisting the urge to squeeze them really hard.

This was *unbelievable*.

Nate watched very carefully.

Unless Alice was using this opportunity to enjoy some free sex with a big-dicked partner, she was going to finish him off any second now.

She bounced vigorously, shaking the car.

Then he saw a glint of metal in her hand.

TWENTY-ONE

Shane pressed his face between Bethany's breasts. He wished she wasn't wearing the dress, because he wanted to feel her bare skin. He tried to pull it down, but it wasn't the kind of dress you could tug down like that, so instead he tried to pull it up.

He hoped she'd help him, maybe yanking the dress up over her head and tossing it to the side, but she didn't. She did, however, bounce even more vigorously.

"You don't have to hold back," she gasped. "Come whenever you're ready."

"You first," he said.

He pulled his face away from her breasts. She had one hand on his shoulder, gripping him so tightly that it almost hurt. In her other hand was—

ALICE LET GO OF SHANE'S SHOULDER AND SLAMMED HER HAND against his chin, pushing his head back.

She thrust the knife at his neck.

BETHANY'S PINKY FINGER WAS PRESSED AGAINST HIS MOUTH, AND Shane bit down on it as hard as he could while twisting his body out of the way. The blade of the knife jabbed deep into his shoulder, and he cried out in pain, giving Bethany the chance to pull her bloody finger out of his mouth.

He punched her in the face.

Bethany fell over, taking the knife with her.

Shane was still inside her. He tried to pull out, but she was still sitting on him despite being flopped over on the seat.

She sat back up and swung the knife at him like a serial killer in a slasher flick.

It sliced across the side of his neck.

He grabbed her hand by the wrist and squeezed, trying to break bones. "Drop it!"

She winced in pain and dropped the knife. It landed on his leg, but handle-side down.

He was completely limp now, and Bethany raised herself enough that he popped free.

Now he was glad she was still wearing her dress because he grabbed her by the back of it and slammed her face into the dashboard, hard enough that he hoped he was shattering teeth. He slammed her into it again and again, at least six or seven times, and then shoved her back onto the driver's seat. Even in the dark, he could see the large streak of blood she'd left behind.

He picked up the knife. The bitch was lucky he didn't stab her to death with it.

Shane got out of the car.

He caught a split-second glimpse of a man—Bethany's ex who'd accosted them at the coffee shop—swinging a baseball bat at his head. It connected, there was an incredible burst of pain, and then everything went black.

Shane dropped to the ground, unconscious.

Nate glanced into the car. Alice was lying on her side, not moving.

He looked at Shane again. The half-naked man was lying on his back. A trickle of blood ran down each side of his mouth, and it looked like...

Yeah, when Nate peered closer, there was blood running out of his left ear.

Oh, shit...had he killed him?

Oh, shit!

Nate crouched down next to him, frantically searching for signs of life.

He didn't seem to be breathing.

Fuck, fuck, fuck!

Nate slapped his cheek. "Shane? Hey, Shane! Wake up, man! Wake up!"

Shane didn't move.

No. No, no, no, no, no. After all this, he couldn't have accidentally killed him. It wasn't possible. That would be too fucked up.

He pressed his thumb against Shane's wrist, feeling for a pulse.

There was nothing.

He'd broken Shane's goddamn neck.

Okay...think.

Think.

Nobody was monitoring Shane's vital signs. Nobody else knew he was dead.

Hell, Alice was inside the car with her necklace. They probably had no idea what was happening out here.

But just in case…

"Oh, thank God!" Nate exclaimed. "Just stay with me, Shane. Stay with me. Don't you die on me. Just hold out a little bit longer."

Nate climbed into the car. There was a *lot* of blood on the dashboard.

He patted Alice on the leg. "Alice? Hey, Alice?"

She didn't move.

"Alice, I really need you to wake up. Please?"

He dragged her out of the car, then gently leaned her against the vehicle. Her head lolled forward.

She was breathing, at least.

"Alice, you have to wake up! You're going to lose everything if you don't! Wake up!"

Could he put the knife in Alice's hand and then move it himself to slice open Shane's throat? That obviously wasn't in the spirit of the game, but would they allow that? Why execute a couple of innocent children just because things went south at the last minute?

He shook Alice by the shoulder.

She raised her head and opened up one swollen eye.

"Alice! Can you hear me?"

She kind of nodded.

Nate pointed to Shane's body. "He's right there. He's in bad shape but he's still alive. You need to finish him off."

Alice opened up her other eye.

Nate gave her the knife.

She crawled over to Shane.

She held the eyeball charm of her necklace up to her mouth.

"You're watching what's happening, right? I'm gonna do it. Pay attention." Her words were difficult to understand, but the gist was clear.

Alice spat out some blood, then raised the knife.

Shane opened his eyes.

Grabbed Alice by the throat.

Shit! This was why Nate was a waiter and not a paramedic!

Alice slammed the knife into Shane's neck.

Nate turned away in horror, though not soon enough to miss the spurt of blood.

He listened to the awful, wet sounds of her slamming the knife into him over and over.

When he looked back over at her, she was still stabbing him.

Nate placed his hand on her arm and took the knife from her. "It's over," he said. "He's gone." His mind felt like it was moving in fast-forward and rewind at the same time. He was never going to recover from this. He was going to end up in a straitjacket, cackling madly in his special padded cell.

"He's gone," said Alice. "*He's gone.*" She picked up the charm again. "It's over! I did it! I won!"

They waited for a moment. What were they supposed to do now?

Nate's phone vibrated in his pocket. He took it out. *Unknown caller.* He pressed the "Accept Call" button but didn't say anything.

"Ms. Vinestalk dropped her phone in the car, so we're calling you," said a man on the other end. It sounded like the guy in the facemask. "Just hang tight for about twenty minutes."

"Okay."

"See you in a bit."

Nate hung up and put the phone back in his pocket. "We're supposed to just hang tight for about twenty minutes," he informed Alice, his voice a soft monotone.

"Okay."

Shane's body was covered in blood and stab wounds, so it probably didn't matter, but Nate thought the guy deserved the dignity of not lying there with his junk on display. After a couple of false starts where he almost passed out, Nate managed to look through Shane's car. He didn't find a blanket or anything he could use to cover him up. Though Nate did have a blanket in the trunk of his own car, he had just enough of his sanity remaining to know it wasn't a very good idea to leave his personal possessions at a crime scene. Shane would just have to deal with it.

Nate and Alice sat there, not speaking. Every once in a while she spat out some blood.

Twenty minutes later, a black van pulled into the park. The man, still wearing that goddamn facemask, got out. He immediately walked over to Shane's corpse and prodded it with his toe.

"Yeah, he's pretty fucking dead. Well done."

"Where are my kids?" Alice demanded.

"Here's the thing. We were going to bring them, but you stabbed this guy, like, three hundred times, and his gigantic cock is on display. My thought is that perhaps you should be reunited with them at a separate location."

"He has a point," said Nate, barely hearing his own voice.

The man handed Nate a piece of paper. "Go to that address. We'll clean everything up."

"You'll clean it up?"

"Sure. It's a friendly service we provide. We'll make poor Shane Flagler go bye-bye."

"So I never needed to help her?"

The man shrugged. "You did your part." He reached into the passenger seat and took out a small Styrofoam cooler. "There are some ice packs, wet towels, and other things in here. Clean yourself up before you see the kids. Now shoo."

Nate thanked him.

They slowly walked back to his car.

"THERE'S A WHOLE FIRST AID KIT IN HERE," SAID ALICE. SHE CUT some gauze with a pair of scissors, and wrapped it around the finger Shane had bitten. He'd took out a seriously big chunk of flesh, but Alice didn't seem too bothered by the pain.

"How do you feel?" Nate asked.

"In shock. It hasn't hit me yet that it's over."

"I mean, how do you feel about what you did?"

"I did what I had to do."

"You killed him." Nate's voice quivered. He could feel himself losing his already very, very tenuous hold of his self-control.

"I know."

"I mean, you stabbed him like a fucking psychopath." It was all hitting Nate at once. They were murderers. Monsters. Did Shane Flagler have people who cared about him? People who loved him? If they were making Shane simply disappear, would they ever get the closure they needed? Would they live the rest of their lives not knowing what happened?

"And you cracked his skull with a bat," said Alice.

"I know! I know what I did!" Nate's heart felt like it was beating a thousand times a minute. This was what a full-on panic attack felt like. "We killed him. He didn't do anything."

"I killed him, not you. And I didn't have a choice. You know that."

"We're gonna get caught."

"No, we aren't."

"We are!"

"No, Nate, we aren't. They're cleaning it up. We're fine."

"Then we need to turn ourselves in! Oh my God! What did we do, Alice? What the fuck did we do?" Nate's whole body began to tremble, and he could barely catch his breath.

"Nate, pull over. Right now. You're in no shape to drive."

Nate pulled off the side of the road, the car jolting as it went over the curb.

"I need you to calm down," said Alice. "Can you calm down for me?"

"No! I work at a Tex-Mex restaurant! I heard his neck break! I saw the blood spray when you stabbed him! How the fuck am I supposed to get that out of my head? How will I ever get that out of my head, Alice?"

"You will. You'll get over it."

"We're going to be looking over our shoulders for the rest of our lives."

"No, we aren't."

"We are. We need to turn ourselves in. We need to get it over with. We need to—"

Nate's mouth dropped open as Alice slammed the scissors deep into his chest.

"I'm so sorry," she said.

"I…"

"You wouldn't listen to me." Alice pulled the scissors out, then stabbed him again. "We won the game. Why did you have to ruin it? Why did you have to make me a widow?"

Nate fell against the steering wheel, honking the horn. Alice pulled him toward her, and the horn stopped.

"I'm going to make sure your play gets produced," she told him. "I promise you that. I'm going to devote all of my energy to making sure the world sees it. Through your art, you'll live forever."

Then she stabbed him once more.

She closed her eyes and took a long, deep breath. She touched the necklace with her bloody fingers.

"If you're still listening," she said, "Could I ask another favor?"

Her phone rang. When she answered, the man assured her that, yes, he'd take care of it.

THE BLACK VAN DROPPED HER OFF IN FRONT OF A SMALL HOUSE.

The front door opened. Olympia and Peter ran outside.

They screamed in joy and ran to Alice, throwing their arms around her.

"I've missed you so much!" Alice told them. "So, so much!"

"Can we go home, Mommy?" asked Peter.

Alice shook her head. "No, honey, we can't go home. We're going far away, but we'll make a new home. And we'll always be together. Just know that Mommy will do anything for you."

She knelt down and hugged her children tight.

"Anything."

— The End —

ACKNOWLEDGMENTS

Thanks to Jamie La Chance, Tod Clark, Donna Fitzpatrick, Lynne Hansen, Michael McBride, Jim Morey, Bridgett Nelson, and Paul Synuria II for their ongoing efforts to try to stop me from looking like a complete dumbass.

ABOUT THE AUTHOR

Follow Jeff's ridiculous musings here:

- facebook.com/JeffStrandAuthorFanPage
- twitter.com/JeffStrand
- instagram.com/jeffstrandauthor
- amazon.com/Jeff-Strand/e/B001K8D3F0

OTHER BOOKS BY JEFF STRAND

Demonic. Corey is in love with his co-worker Quinn. Quinn's husband is a savage serial killer. When Corey decides to help her out by trying to murder her husband, things do not quite work out as he hoped.

Freaky Briefs. A collection of 75 flash fiction stories.

The Writing Life: Reflections, Recollections, and a Lot of Cursing. A comedic (but entirely true) non-fiction book about surviving in a brutal business.

Candy Coated Madness. Another demented collection of gleefully macabre tales.

Autumn Bleeds Into Winter. A coming-of-age thriller set in Fairbanks, Alaska in 1979. Fourteen-year-old Curtis saw his best friend get abducted, and he's going to confront the man who did it.

The Odds. When invited to a game that offers a 99% chance of winning fifty thousand dollars, Ethan rejoices at the chance to recoup his gambling losses. But as the game continues, the odds constantly change, and the risks become progressively deadlier...

Allison. She can break your bones using her mind. And she's trying very hard not to hurt you.

Wolf Hunt 3. George, Lou, Ally, and Eugene are back in another werewolf-laden adventure.

Clowns Vs. Spiders. Choose your side!

My Pretties. A serial kidnapper may have met his match in the two young ladies who walk the city streets at night, using themselves as bait...

Five Novellas. A compilation of *Stalking You Now, An Apocalypse of Our Own, Faint of Heart, Kutter,* and *Facial.*

Ferocious. The creatures of the forest are dead...and hungry!

Bring Her Back. A tale of revenge and madness.

Sick House. A home invasion from beyond the grave.

Bang Up. A filthy comedic thriller. "You want to pay me to sleep with your wife?" is just the start of the story.

Cold Dead Hands. Ten people are trapped in a freezer during a terrorist attack on a grocery store.

How You Ruined My Life (Young Adult). Sixteen-year-old Rod has a pretty cool life until his cousin Blake moves in and slowly destroys everything he holds dear.

Everything Has Teeth. A third collection of short tales of horror and macabre comedy.

An Apocalypse of Our Own. Can the Friend Zone survive the end of the world?

Stranger Things Have Happened (Young Adult). Teenager Marcus Millian III is determined to be one of the greatest magicians who ever lived. Can he make a live shark disappear from a tank?

Cyclops Road. When newly widowed Evan Portin gives a woman named Harriett a ride out of town, she says she's on a cross-country journey to slay a Cyclops. Is she crazy, or...?

Blister. While on vacation, cartoonist Jason Tray meets the town legend, a hideously disfigured woman who lives in a shed.

The Greatest Zombie Movie Ever (Young Adult). Three best friends with more passion than talent try to make the ultimate zombie epic.

Kumquat. A road trip comedy about TV, hot dogs, death, and obscure fruit.

I Have a Bad Feeling About This (Young Adult). Geeky, non-athletic Henry Lambert is sent to survival camp, which is bad enough *before* the trio of murderous thugs show up.

Pressure. What if your best friend was a killer...and he wanted you to be just like him? Bram Stoker Award nominee for Best Novel.

Dweller. The lifetime story of a boy and his monster. Bram Stoker Award nominee for Best Novel.

A Bad Day For Voodoo. A young adult horror/comedy about why sticking pins in a voodoo doll of your history teacher isn't always the best idea. Bram Stoker Award nominee for Best Young Adult Novel.

Dead Clown Barbecue. A collection of demented stories about severed noses, ventriloquist dummies, giant-sized vampires, sibling stabbings, and lots of other messed-up stuff.

Dead Clown Barbecue Expansion Pack. A few more stories for those who couldn't get enough.

Wolf Hunt. Two thugs for hire. One beautiful woman. And one vicious frickin' werewolf.

Wolf Hunt 2. New wolf. Same George and Lou.

The Sinister Mr. Corpse. The feel-good zombie novel of the year.

Benjamin's Parasite. A rather disgusting action/horror/comedy about why getting infected with a ghastly parasite is unpleasant.

Fangboy. A dark and demented fairy tale for adults.

Facial. Greg has just killed the man he hired to kill one of his wife's many lovers. Greg's brother desperately needs a dead body. It's kind of related to the lion corpse that he found in his basement. This is the normal part of the story.

Kutter. A serial killer finds a Boston terrier, and it might just make him into a better person.

Faint of Heart. To get her kidnapped husband back, Melody has to relive her husband's nightmarish weekend, step-by-step...and survive.

Mandibles. Giant killer ants wreaking havoc in the big city!

Stalking You Now. A twisty-turny thriller soon to be the feature film *Mindy Has To Die.*

Graverobbers Wanted (No Experience Necessary). First in the Andrew Mayhem series.

Single White Psychopath Seeks Same. Second in the Andrew Mayhem series.

Casket For Sale (Only Used Once). Third in the Andrew Mayhem series.

Lost Homicidal Maniac (Answers to "Shirley"). Fourth in the Andrew Mayhem series.

Cemetery Closing (Everything Must Go). Fifth in the Andrew Mayhem series.

Suckers (with JA Konrath). Andrew Mayhem meets Harry McGlade. Which one will prove to be more incompetent?

Gleefully Macabre Tales. A collection of thirty-two demented tales. Bram Stoker Award nominee for Best Collection.

Elrod McBugle on the Loose. A comedy for kids (and adults who were warped as kids).

The Haunted Forest Tour (with Jim Moore). The greatest theme park attraction in the world! Take a completely safe ride through an actual haunted forest! Just hope that your tram doesn't break down, because this forest is PACKED with monsters...

Draculas (with JA Konrath, Blake Crouch, and F. Paul Wilson). An outbreak of feral vampires in a secluded hospital. This one isn't much like *Twilight*.

For information on all of these books, visit Jeff Strand's more-or-less official website at http://www.JeffStrand.com

Subscribe to Jeff Strand's free monthly newsletter (which includes a brand-new original short story in every issue) at http://eepurl.com/bpv5br

And remember:

Readers who leave reviews deserve great big hugs!

Made in United States
Orlando, FL
09 August 2023

35897688R00157